It's already getting colder, even out here in the desert. When the sun goes out for good, I imagine it's gonna get seriously cold real fast. Being underground might be a little bit warmer.

"Like the government's going to let just anybody into Yucca Mountain. I don't hear anything about the President going to Yucca Mountain. That guy who ran against him—he's probably going to Yucca Mountain." Maude makes rude noise and takes a clothespin out of her jeans pocket. "You really want to live down there where they want to put all that nuclear waste?"

No, I don't. I never did trust the government's plan to bury the nation's nuclear garbage practically in my back yard. Seemed rude somehow, considering no one ever asked me how I felt about it.

"I heard the Lehman Caves have bats," Maude says. Maude don't like bats, calls 'em rats with wings.

Together Maude and I pin another sheet on the line.

"You don't seem altogether too upset about this," I say after a minute.

—from "One Sun, No Waiting"

Eight From the Silver State

Nevada Stories by

ANNIE REED

TVP

Thunder Valley Press

EIGHT FROM THE SILVER STATE

"Introduction" by Annie Reed, Copyright November, 2011
"Night Passage" by Annie Reed, Copyright 2011
"Lady of the Deep" by Annie Reed, Copyright 2011
"One Sun, No Waiting" by Annie Reed, Copyright 2011
"Bait" by Annie Reed, Copyright 2011
"Night of the Cruisers" by Annie Reed, Copyright 2011
"For a Few Lattes More" by Annie Reed, first published in
  The Trouble with Heroes, Daw Books, 2009
"Strike Two" by Annie Reed, Copyright 2011
"Love Among the Llamas" by Annie Reed, Copyright 2011

Published by Thunder Valley Press
www.thundervalleypress.com

Cover art copyright © Sly5800 | Dreamstime.com
Book and cover design copyright © Thunder Valley Press

ISBN: 0615822398
ISBN-13: 978-0615822396

Eight From the Silver State

Nevada Stories by

ANNIE REED

CONTENTS

INTRODUCTION

The other night when I was reviewing the stories for this collection, I started thinking about a song I learned as a kid: "Home Means Nevada," which my Internet research says was written by Bertha Rafetto, and which I know was sung by the student body at almost every assembly during my elementary school years.

Yes, I'm a Nevada native. We do exist, unlike the jackalope. My husband's a Nevada native, too, and since we're both life-long residents of the Silver State, so is our daughter. That means we live in a state that's mostly desert, a large chunk of which is owned by the federal government. The politics are conservative, gambling is legal, and so is prostitution in counties where more jackrabbits live than people, although I don't think that's a prerequisite.

Like me, the stories in this collection were born and raised in Nevada, so to speak. They encompass a wide variety of genres, from women's fiction to horror, science fiction to romance. There's even a couple of mob stories thrown in for good measure. I mean, this *is* Nevada. How could there not be a mob story?

What was it like growing up in Nevada? Well, there were slot machines in the grocery stores where my parents shopped, for one thing. There were also slot machines in the bowling alley and the Laundromat. Casinos were just a part of the landscape, as were the cattle that spent the winters in a large field behind the house where I spent my middle grade and high school years. That field's part of a business park now, and the next field over, where a farmer used to grow garlic, is home to an enclosed mall.

This summer I attended WorldCon in Reno. One of the panels I attended focused on using Nevada as a setting. It was interesting to hear writers I admire talk about the oddities of my state—the vast open areas where a person can find themselves totally alone; the fact that residents carry water with us when we drive because we're aware we live in a desert; the fact that a simple walk in the hills might bring an unwary hiker face-to-face with a rattlesnake.

While I've never come face-to-face with a rattle-snake, the drive across miles and miles and *miles* of desert to get from one town to the next, often on roads with no other cars in sight for hours at a time, is some-thing I tend to take for granted. I don't think about the danger. At least, not while I'm driving.

The first story in this collection, "Night Passage," is about a mother and daughter making the long drive from Las Vegas to Reno at night. They don't think about the danger of being alone in a desert either, not until the hazards of the road force both of them to face truths they'd rather not think about.

"Lady of the Deep" is set in a fictionalized version of a place I've come to know well. Part of the reason I've never faced an angry rattlesnake in the hills behind my house is that I do my walking around the perimeter of a man-made marina. One Saturday morning after our walk, my husband and I spent time watching competitive sandcastle builders do their thing on the beach at the marina. That night I started writing "Lady of the Deep," inspired by one of the elaborate sand sculptures I watched being created that day.

The next story in this collection, "One Sun, No

Waiting," is set in a small, blink-and-you'd-miss-it town outside of Las Vegas. Two-thirds of the population of Nevada lives in the Las Vegas metro area, but once the lights of Vegas fade in the rearview mirror, the desert is dry and dusty and hugely empty. It takes a special kind of person to call a small desert town home. "One Sun, No Waiting" is a near-future science fiction story about two of those people.

My daughter is a huge zombie fan. While I've watched most of the movies in her zombie DVD collection, I wasn't that big a fan myself. Then I got hooked on AMC's *The Walking Dead.* I can't remember ever being that tense throughout every episode of a television show before in my life. It wasn't the zombies that hooked me, though; it was the story of the survivors. As of the date I'm writing this introduction, I've written five zombie stories, and I'm certain there will be more. The zombie story in this collection—"Bait"—features people who, through skill or just plain dumb luck, manage to survive attacks by the infected. The question becomes whether the uninfected can survive each other.

"Night of the Cruisers" was inspired by my daily commute. I tend to watch people, as a lot of writers do, which means I pay attention to the cars on the road with me. When I started noting an inordinately high percentage of P.T. Cruisers along my usual route, I began thinking about why there were so many of that particular car on the road. I'd hoped writing the story would exorcise the things, but I'm still seeing them in ever-increasing numbers. I may have to write a second story just to see what happens.

I wrote the next story in this collection, "For a Few Lattes More," for an anthology edited by Denise Little. While many of the stories in the anthology featured well-known mythic heroes, I wrote about a different kind of hero: the cowboy without a name from the spaghetti Westerns my dad used to watch when I was a kid. Since the anthology centered on stories where the hero's armor is a little on the tarnished side, suffice it to say that my take on the cowboy without a name is a bit different than Clint Eastwood's.

"Strike Two" is the second of the mob-related stories in this book. No, I'm not telling which story is the other mob story; you'll have to read them to find out.

The last story in this collection is "Love Among the Llamas." When I started writing this story, I had no idea it was a romance. I thought it was simply a story about a woman who breaks free of her routine. Then Mr. Right made his appearance, and the light bulb went off. It's funny how fiction works out that way sometimes.

I hope you enjoy the stories in this collection. I enjoy writing short fiction as well as longer works, and as long as Thunder Valley Press is willing to put together these themed collections, I'm more than happy to keep writing the stories.

—Annie Reed
Reno, Nevada
November 9, 2011

NIGHT PASSAGE

The road stretched in front of Joleen, a dark ribbon in the darker night. Something glittered on the asphalt ahead of her, but she couldn't tell if her car's headlights reflected off pieces of quartz or broken glass. Either one was a possibility. Even this far out in the desert broken beer bottles littered the sides of the road, twentieth century man's way of marking his territory.

Casey sat in the passenger seat pretending total interest in the ghostly shapes flying by her window. Joleen could tell her daughter still was angry by the tense set of her shoulders and the way she kept her face turned away from her mother.

Joleen steered around the mess on the road as best

she could on the narrow, two-lane highway. She hoped it wasn't glass. The tires on her car were old and worn, and she was afraid glass would go right through them. The bright lights of Las Vegas had faded to a dim glow on the horizon far behind her, and Goldfield was at least 40 miles to the north. She didn't want to have to stop out here in the middle of nowhere to fix a flat, especially not at night. Except for gas, she didn't want to stop at all until she got to Reno.

"Are you hungry?" Joleen asked just for something to say.

Casey didn't respond. No one could do the silent treatment better than an angry thirteen-year-old girl.

"Because if you are, we've got snacks and sodas in the back seat," Joleen said, trying again.

A sigh. Not much, but it was a chink in the armor, something Joleen could work with. It would be a long, long drive if Casey decided to stay angry the whole way.

Maybe a little music would help.

"Why don't you find something to listen to?" Joleen fumbled for the tape case without taking her eyes off the road. "We're can't pick up a station out here, and if you're not going to talk to me, then I need something to keep me company."

This time she got the rolled-eyes, *oh Mom* look, but

her daughter took the tapes and rummaged through them.

"I know you didn't want to move," Joleen said.

"Look, Mom, I don't want to talk about it," Casey said, slamming the tape case shut. "Like my opinion would mean anything anyway," she added under her breath. Thirteen-year-olds always added something under their breath, that first sign of future rebellion.

Joleen took a deep breath. "So what do you want to talk about?"

Casey popped the tape in and turned back toward the window. "Nothing," she said. "I don't want to talk about anything, okay?"

So much for that plan.

Rock music blared from the speakers. Obviously one of Casey's tapes. Joleen didn't know the name of the band, but at least it might keep her awake. If she didn't go deaf first.

Thirty seconds later, Joleen reached for the volume control. She actually liked most rock music but that last guitar riff made her fillings vibrate. She glanced down at the tape deck to make sure she found the right knob.

"Mom, look out!"

Joleen jerked her eyes back to the road. She caught a glimpse of a large animal right in front of them.

Heart in her throat, Joleen spun the wheel hard to the left and slammed on the brakes.

Not good. She made it past the cow—she could see now that it was a cow—without hitting it, but the car started to skid, tires squealing. The rear end of the car slid around toward the front, threatening to send them into a spin.

Joleen turned the wheel back to the right and took her foot off the brake, praying that the car would right itself.

That's when the tire blew.

Casey screamed again.

The steering wheel jerked in Joleen's hands as the car pulled in the direction of the blowout and onto the wrong side of the highway. Joleen struggled as hard as she could to control it, muscles straining, but trying to turn the wheel was like yanking on a jar lid that didn't want to budge.

"Help me!" When Casey didn't move, Joleen yelled louder. *"Help me!"*

Casey jumped but she grabbed the wheel, her hands next to Joleen's, and pulled. With the two of them working at it they managed to turn the car back onto the right side of the road, the left front wheel thumping as what was left of the tire shredded under the rim.

"Aim for the side of the road," Joleen said, and together they steered the car off the asphalt. Once the tires hit the soft dirt of the shoulder, the car slowed down. Joleen feathered the brakes until the car shuddered to a stop.

Casey jerked her hands off the steering wheel like it was molten metal and sat back in her seat, her face white and pasty in the reflected light of the dashboard.

Joleen let out a long, shuddering breath and rested her head on the steering wheel between her hands. She wasn't ready to let go of the wheel just yet. She was shaking badly, and she didn't want Casey to know just how frightened she'd been. So instead Joleen sat with her eyes closed and let the delayed stress reaction work its way through her.

After a few minutes, Joleen felt Casey's light touch on her shoulder. "Mom?" Casey asked, her voice small and tentative. "Are you okay, Mom?"

Joleen took a deep breath and raised her head to look at her daughter. She forced a smile. "Yeah, I'm okay. I've got a few more gray hairs than I did a minute ago, but I'm okay."

Casey didn't buy it for a minute, Joleen could tell. She took one hand off the steering wheel and brushed a strand of hair off Casey's face. "How about you?"

Casey flinched away. "I'm fine," she said in a tight, clipped voice, turning her face back toward the window as she reached up to rearrange her hair.

Joleen should have known better. Casey didn't like it when her mom tried to fix her hair. But Joleen had hoped Casey would make an exception, just this once, for her sake. Right now Joleen needed her daughter, the one who used to share chair with her so they could cuddle watching television, not this angry adolescent stranger.

"You're fine, I'm fine, I guess the only thing that isn't fine is the car," Joleen said, suddenly very angry herself. "I'm going to go look at the tire."

Joleen heard Casey's muttered "fine" as she shut the door behind herself.

"Fine!" Joleen said, venting a little of her own anger at the night.

Joleen took a flashlight from the trunk and walked around to the front of the car. The tire on the driver's side was a wreck.

"Dammit," Joleen said. Not only was the tire shredded to ribbons, the rim was bent. They would have to spend the night in Goldfield, or Tonopah if she could make it that far on her car's small emergency spare, and then hope that when the service stations opened in the morning, someone would have a wheel that would fit. At least she'd remembered to check the spare before they left.

Of course, the jack and the spare were buried under all the stuff jammed in the trunk. Once Joleen realized they had to move back to Reno, she sold or gave away a lot of their things, which didn't make Casey any happier about the move. What was left was either packed in the car or placed in storage.

Joleen stood with her hands on her hips, staring at the open trunk. It didn't look this full when they left.

She walked around to the passenger side and knocked on Casey's window. After a minute Casey rolled it down. "I could use some help," Joleen said.

Casey got out without a word and trailed along behind Joleen to the back of the car.

Joleen nodded at the open trunk. "We need to unload all this so I can get the spare."

"You've got to be kidding me. Mom, it took us forever to get it all in there! And where are we going to put it?"

Casey's whining was the last thing she needed. Especially now.

Not trusting herself to answer, Joleen hefted a suitcase out of the trunk and set it on the shoulder of the road behind the car.

Casey stared at her, her mouth open in disbelief. "You're just going to put all our stuff in the dirt?"

"If you have a better idea, go for it," Joleen said, grabbing a shopping bag full of shoes. "At this point I don't care, I just want to change the tire and get out of here."

Joleen dropped the bag next to the suitcase. She watched Casey out of the corner of her eye as she stood there. That was another thing about thirteen-year-olds. Most of the time they did what you asked, just not immediately.

Finally Casey slung a duffel bag over her shoulder, picked up a box, and walked around to the driver's side of the car. She put the bag on the floor next to the ped-dles and the box on the seat.

"Hey!" Joleen said. "That's my—"

"You're going to be changing the tire, not driving. Why can't I put it there?"

Joleen had to admit she had a point. "Good idea," she said.

Casey walked back to the trunk and lifted out another duffel bag. "You say that like you're surprised. I'm not a baby anymore, Mom. I can figure stuff out."

Joleen dropped a heavy box of dishes on the

shoulder. "I never said you were a baby."

"That's the way you treat me." Casey's face was carefully neutral, but she was concentrating a little too hard on picking up a suitcase out of the trunk. Joleen recognized the look. For Casey, this was about more than just figuring out where to put things.

"If I did, I didn't mean to," Joleen said, choosing her words carefully. "I know you're not a baby anymore."

"Then why don't I get a say in where we live?"

"Casey..."

Casey looked up from the trunk, her eyes angry and accusing. "And why do we have to move, anyway? It's not fair. You get to make all the decisions but you won't tell me why."

They were back to that. This time it was Joleen's turn to look away. "It's complicated, Casey," she said, staring out at the desert. Joleen tried to pick out shapes beyond the reach of the narrow flashlight beam. She wondered if she should be worried about coyotes.

"See, that's just what I mean!" Casey said. "You act like what I think or what I want or what I feel doesn't matter. You treat me like a baby!" Joleen heard Casey sniffle and realized she was crying. "I'm not a baby, Mom. I'm not."

Joleen looked back at her daughter. It could have

been a trick of the light, the open trunk light and flashlight casting strange shadows, or maybe it was because Joleen knew they could have both been killed if the car had rolled when the tire blew, but Casey looked different somehow. Older. Standing there wiping her nose with an angry swipe of her arm, tears spilling down her cheeks, Casey no longer reminded Joleen of the baby she'd held in her arms, the baby who used to keep her up all night wanting to play. That curious double exposure Joleen always saw whenever she looked at her, a blending of Casey then and Casey now, wasn't there anymore.

Joleen felt something inside break as she realized her baby girl was gone forever. She looked down at the ground. She needed to begin letting go. Life was going to be difficult for both of them in the next few months. Casey was going to need to grow up fast, and Joleen had to let her.

Now was as good a time as any to start.

"You're right," Joleen said when she trusted her voice again.

"What?" Casey asked around a sniffle.

Joleen handed Casey a tissue she'd stuffed in the pocket of her jeans, then lifted out the last suitcase and bag between her and the well where the spare tire and jack were hidden. "Don't look so surprised. I said you were right." She dropped the luggage behind her and lifted up the false bottom of the trunk. "Here, can you hold this for me?"

Casey held up the fiberboard panel covering the spare and looked at Joleen like she'd suddenly sprouted antenna or a bushy tail.

Joleen spun the nut holding the spare loose. "I think I just had an epiphany, that's all," she said.

"Epiphany?" Casey echoed, wiping her nose again. "I never heard you use that word before, Mom. Are you sure you're okay?"

Joleen laughed a little. "Don't worry, your mom hasn't gone off the deep end. Wasn't that word on one of your vocabulary lists last year?" With a grunt, Joleen lifted the spare out of the trunk and leaned it against the back bumper. "Anyway, I remember it from somewhere and I think it fits." She stared down at the scissor jack. "I just hope I remember how this thing works," she muttered, picking up the pieces.

Joleen took the jack and lug wrench to the front of the car. She crouched down and aimed the flashlight beam underneath the car. She heard Casey drop the panel back in place, and the next thing she knew Casey had rolled the spare up next to her.

"What are you doing?" Casey asked.

"Looking for the frame," Joleen said. "You can't put a jack just anywhere, not on a car this old. If it's in the wrong place it'll bend the metal instead of lifting the car."

"Can I see?"

Joleen hesitated only a moment. "Sure," she said. Casey bent down next to her, twisting her body around until she could see where Joleen was pointing the light. "That's the frame," Joleen said.

"So the jack goes like this?" Casey asked, sliding it underneath the car.

"Yeah, just like that." Joleen held the jack in place and turned the handle until she felt it snug up against the frame. "Now this is the fun part."

"Fun?"

"Lug nuts." Joleen popped off the hubcap. Fitting the wrench on the first nut, Joleen jerked down hard on the cross-bar. The nut didn't budge. "They put these things on with air guns," she said. "Sometimes this is a real pain." It took her three tries to break the nut loose.

One down, four to go.

"How come you're not taking them all the way off?" Casey asked.

"All I want to do is loosen them up a bit." Joleen

went to work on the next nut. "If I wait until I jack up the car to do this, the tire would just spin and you'd have to hold it for me. And if I take them all the way off now, the tire might shift and bend the bolts. It's just easier this way."

Casey was quiet for a moment. "Did Dad teach you how to do this?" she finally asked.

"No, not your dad. He was never very good with cars."

"Then who did?"

Joleen smiled. It had been so long ago, she'd nearly forgotten. "When I first started to date, I went out with a guy named Mike." She broke the last nut free without a problem. "Mike loved two things in life and one of them was cars. I was just learning how to drive and Mike thought I needed to learn how to change a flat. Guess he was right."

Joleen put down the lug wrench and started cranking the jack handle, grunting with the effort as the jack slowly scissored up and lifted the wheel off the ground.

Casey grinned at her. "You said two things. You were the other one, right, Mom?"

"Me?" Joleen shook her head. "No, the other thing Mike loved was himself. We didn't date for very long."

Joleen stepped back, wiping her hands on her jeans

and trying to judge whether the car was high enough to put on the spare. She thought it might be, but she gave the jack handle an extra turn just in case.

"Sounds like he was a jerk," Casey said. "A useful jerk, but still a jerk."

"It was a long time ago. I'm just glad he taught me about cars."

"Yeah. Me, too."

Joleen spun the lug nuts all the way off and put them in the hubcap like Mike taught her, and then it hit her. That was the first time she'd talked to Casey about anyone she'd dated other than Casey's dad, and even those conversations had been vague, heavy on half-remembered good times, light on reality. The good old days hadn't been all that good and Joleen always thought Casey didn't need to know that. But talking to her about Mike just now had been so easy and natural, it made Joleen wonder. Maybe she'd been wrong about that. Maybe she'd been wrong about a lot of things.

"Mom?"

"What?" Joleen lifted the heavy wheel and what was left of the tire off the car. The rim was useless and she thought about leaving it off the side of the road but decided against it. She wasn't about to add any more trash to the landscape.

"What did you mean when you said you had an epiphany?"

She glanced at Casey. Her daughter was drawing designs in the dirt with the toe of her tennis shoe, staring intently down at her artwork.

Joleen almost said "nothing, really" but stopped herself. That was the answer she'd have given Casey yesterday. It wasn't the right answer now.

"It's just that I realized something kind of important," she said finally. "Something that made me look at things a little differently."

Joleen rolled the spare in place and lifted it up, adjusting it until the bolts threaded through the holes. It was so small, it looked silly hanging there. When she first learned how to do this, spares were full size just like other tires, not like these emergency spares.

"Anyway, what I realized is that whenever I looked at you, a part of me still saw the way you looked when your dad and I brought you home from the hospital, how cute you were in your first Halloween costume, or how you cried your first day of school. And maybe, without even realizing it, I was still treating you like that little girl who refused to take naps in kindergarten and who thought Bobby McNeil was the coolest boy in first grade because he had a pet tarantula."

"Bobby McNeil was a dork," Casey said. "And his tarantula gave me the creeps."

"You say that now, but back then..." She glanced over at her daughter, checking to see if the tease was working. Casey stood there glaring at her, but at least it was a glare without venom.

"The point is, I realized you're growing up and all those memories should stay just that, memories." Joleen threaded the first lug nut back on its bolt, turning it until it made contact with the rim. "In a couple of years you're going to be learning how to drive one of these things, you're going to be making more and more decisions on your own, and as much as I need my little girl sometimes..."

Joleen stopped, uncomfortably aware that all of sudden her voice was unsteady. She concentrated on replacing the rest of the lug nuts, trying to give herself time to get her emotions under control.

Casey stood and watched her, not saying anything for the longest time. "So why did we leave, mom?" she finally asked in a voice almost too soft for Joleen to hear.

Joleen stared at the tire without really seeing it. None of her old responses would work, not anymore. Casey was right, it was her life, too. She deserved to know why.

"I need to go home, Casey," she said.

Such a simple answer, and so very complicated a response.

"But Las Vegas is home! That's where we've always lived."

"That's where you've always lived." Joleen turned the jack handle, letting the car down slowly. "I moved there when I married your dad because that's where he was going to school, but it never felt like home to me, especially not since he died."

Casey frowned at her. "That was a long time ago."

"Yes. Yes, it was," Joleen agreed.

"So why now? You waited this long, why now?"

Joleen pulled the jack out from under the car and realized her hands were shaking. She had hoped this conversation could have waited, waited until Casey was a little older, waited until she figured out how to tell her. Waited until she could figure out how to come to terms with it herself without falling apart.

She still couldn't quite bring herself to say it. Not out loud, not to her daughter. That would make it too real, and she couldn't handle that.

"We don't have anyone in Las Vegas, Casey," Joleen said slowly. "Any family or close friends. Anyone I can trust to take care of you."

"Why would you need anyone to..."

And then Casey knew, Joleen could see it in her face. She was a smart girl, and she was right. She could figure things out.

"You lied to me, Mom," Casey said. "You're not okay, are you? Are you?"

Joleen couldn't stand to look at her daughter, at the pain and anger and betrayal she saw on Casey's face, but Joleen wouldn't let herself look away. "I am, for now. And I plan to be for a long time."

Casey glared at her. "What is it?" she asked, her tone daring her mother to lie to her again. "Or am I not old enough to know?"

It was real. Joleen had to say it, name it, face it. She couldn't hide from the truth by running away to her childhood home. The only home that really mattered was standing right in front of her.

"Cancer," Joleen said, barely getting the word out. "I have cancer."

Casey's anger dissolved. Joleen saw it melt off her face as shock took over. Casey stood there for a moment, looking scared and miserable, and then she threw herself into Joleen's arms. Joleen held her daughter while she cried, telling her not to worry, that everything would be okay. Gradually Joleen realized that Casey was telling her the same thing.

Joleen didn't know how long they stood there, but eventually Casey quieted and she pulled away. Her hair hung in her face, wet strands plastered to her cheeks. Joleen brushed it back before she could stop herself. "Sorry," she said, trying to smile. "I forgot."

"It's okay, Mom," Casey said, wiping her face and pushing her hair behind her ears. "Just don't make a habit of it, okay?"

"Deal."

Casey looked at her a moment longer then bent to pick up the hubcap. "So this goes back on now, right?" she asked.

"Almost." Joleen realized her own face was wet. She wiped it dry with the back of her hand. "First we have to make sure the lug nuts are really tight, then we can put the hubcap back on."

Casey put the hubcap down and picked up the wrench. "Show me how," she said.

LADY OF THE DEEP

A sandcastle competition.   At a man-made lake
where the sand had to be carted in on dump trucks
because the lake used to be a rock quarry, and the last
thing those beaches had was any natural sand. Greg had
never heard of anything sillier, except maybe the fact
that Sylvia wanted to watch the competition.

"It's a hundred degrees out there," Greg said. "And
you want to stand around and watch grown men play in
the dirt."

The two of them were sitting in Sylvia's battered old
Honda. The parking lot at the public entrance to the
lake was only half-full even though it was the second
Saturday in July and the swimming was free, which

meant the place should have been swarming with kids. Even little kids had sense enough to stay inside out of the sun.

"Aw, c'mon," Sylvia said. "It'll be fun. We have sunscreen and an umbrella and a blanket in the back, and I bet they're selling beer and hotdogs. It'll be just like a picnic. Didn't you ever go on a picnic?"

"No."

Well, that wasn't quite true, but Sylvia wouldn't know that. They'd only been dating a few weeks. Sylvia was great in bed and easy to look at, even if she wasn't exactly what Greg would call pretty, but she had this thing about being outdoors. She liked to just sit outside and watch the world go by. Sometimes she liked to go on walks. Like on the concrete path around the outside of this particular lake.

"You need the fresh air," she said.

Okay, sure, he worked in a cubicle farm all day, and left on his own, he'd play video games all night, but was that any reason to make him bake in the sun on the hottest day of the year?

"And if you've never been on a picnic..." Sylvia let the thought hang in the air, like she wanted him to finish it. When he didn't, she said, "Well, we really need to go on a little picnic of our own, then." She leaned over the center console and kissed him. "You can rub sunscreen all over me." She arched one eyebrow and kissed him again. "And I can rub sunscreen all over you."

Greg had a vision of Sylvia naked. She did look pretty good with her clothes off. And rubbing on sunscreen was a legitimate way of touching her in public without anyone raising a fuss.

"Then you can rub me more, later," she said, her mouth up by his ear.

"Okay," he said, thinking—not for the first time—that men did the stupidest things just to get laid.

The lake wasn't all that big. The concrete walkway that circled the water was exactly two miles around. Greg knew that because signs counted off every half-mile to encourage couch potatoes like him to *Keep On Walking!* He could almost see the little smiley face that should have been at the bottom of each sign.

The lake also had a distinct lack of shade. The few trees the city had planted when they got the brilliant idea to turn the former quarry into a lake were all along one quarter-mile stretch on the south side. The sandcastle competition was on a little peninsula between the main body of the lake and a shallow cove where kids were allowed to swim. Of course, there were no trees to speak of on the peninsula, and it turned out that Sylvia's umbrella wasn't a big beach umbrella but one made to keep the rain off just one person. If that person was a dwarf.

"I'm gonna get fried," Greg said as Sylvia spread out the blanket on a patch of lawn that was half grass and half weeds and more than half baked by the sun. He'd worn his only pair of shorts, and his legs were fish-belly white.

"We have plenty of sunscreen," Sylvia said.

The city was giving out free samples of sunscreen at a little booth at the base of the peninsula, no doubt in an attempt to avoid liability for third-degree burns at a city-sponsored event. Planting a few more trees would have made more sense, but hey—nobody ever said politicians had any sense or they wouldn't have run for office to begin with.

"I don't see anyone selling beer," Greg said.

In fact, the city had posted signs prohibiting alcohol consumption at the lake.

"That truck's selling hotdogs," Sylvia said, pointing at a dilapidated food truck parked next to a band stand. Music was blaring from two banks of speakers, and a drum set on stage promised live music later for those who managed to escape heat exhaustion.

Sylvia patted the blanket next to where she sat. Greg plopped down beside her and was promptly poked in the butt by a dried out weed.

He was starting to rethink exactly how much he'd be willing to put up with just to get laid. Initially Sylvia had told him she just wanted to go for a walk, but ever since she'd hauled out the blanket and the umbrella and the whole impromptu picnic idea, he had the sneaking suspicion she'd planned the whole thing. The least she could have done was warn him so he could have brought a hat or worn long pants. His shins were already turning blotchy red in the sun.

"So why again are we here?" Greg asked.

She pointed toward the beach. "Sandcastles," she said. "I've never watched anyone build a really fancy one, have you?"

On the other side of a short concrete retaining wall, three men were working on tall mounds of sand. When Sylvia first mentioned sandcastles, Greg had envisioned castle-like shapes made of blocks of sand packed into buckets, with vague doors and windows carved in the sides and maybe a paper flag poked on top. What the men on the beach were doing was creating sculptures made of hard-packed sand.

The guy on the left looked like he was barely getting started. Most of the sand for his sculpture was still inside wooden forms that looked for all the world like giant-sized versions of the layer cake pans Greg's mom used to use.

The sculptor in the middle was further along on his sandcastle, although it wasn't a castle either. He'd carved his mound of sand into a sailing ship. Four huge sails soared above a wooden hull, and it looked like he was working on creating waves now at the bottom of the boat.

But it was the sculpture on the right that caught Greg's attention. At first he thought the guy was building a mountain like Richard Dreyfuss's character had with mashed potatoes in that old science fiction movie Greg's parents used to like. Then the guy moved off to the side, and Greg saw it wasn't a mountain. The sculptor was creating a woman.

She was beautiful.

Greg sat forward on the blanket, the pokey weeds forgotten.

It didn't matter that the woman's face was made of wet sand. Her cheeks were round, her lips full, her mouth tilted up in a gentle smile. The parts of the sculpture that Greg had thought were sides of a mountain were really the long, flowing strands of her hair. The same brilliant sun that had made Greg squint even behind his sunglasses created deep shadows in the hollows the sculptor had carved for her eyes. Greg could imagine kindness in those shadows.

He stood up. "I want to get a closer look," he said.

"I thought you weren't all that interested," Sylvia said.

He shrugged. "You coming?"

She leaned back on the blanket. Apparently the weeds only poked him. "I'm just going to sit here a while. Soak up the sun."

Greg's shirt was already soaked through. Sylvia claimed to like the heat, the hotter the better. He had a sinking suspicion she wasn't quite right in the head.

She was good in bed, though.

"I'll bring you back frozen yogurt," he said. There was a frozen yogurt truck next to the hotdog truck. Sylvia liked the stuff, though Greg had no idea why. He was an ice cream man, himself.

She smiled at him. "Thanks, sweetie."

Greg tried not to wince. His mom used to call him sweetie when he was little, and he hadn't liked it much then, either.

He thought the illusion of beauty might fade once he got close to the sculpture of the woman.

It didn't.

The sculptor was crafting the woman three times life

size. At that scale, the grains of sand looked like fine powder on her face, especially now that the heat was drying the outer layer to a light tan. The effect gave her hair highlights, and the deep pools of her eyes, where the sand was still wet, looked even more dramatic.

This was the kind of woman Greg would be more than willing to take a lot of crap from just to spend time with. He wouldn't even have to have sex with her, although he imagined she'd make him feel better than any other woman ever could.

"Impressive, isn't she?" said a man standing next to Greg.

Greg glanced sideways. The man was in his fifties, easy. He had a beer gut his loose tee shirt did nothing to disguise and a double chin, and a stupid little straw hat on his sunburned head. Like Greg, he had on plaid shorts, but unlike Greg, his legs were deeply tanned, just like his arms.

"Yeah," Greg said. Then, just to be conversational, he asked, "Who's she supposed to be, anyway? You know?"

"You mean you don't?"

"The lady of the lake," said another man, this one behind Greg.

Greg turned around. This guy could have been a

twin to the old guy with the beer gut and the straw hat, only he was wearing a bucket hat that had seen better days, and he was carrying a fishing pole.

"Wasn't that a fairy tale?" Greg wasn't all that up on his fairy tales. High school English classes were thankfully far enough behind him that the details of the various stories they'd studied were fuzzy in his brain.

"Legend," Bucket Hat said. "They're all legends."

"Yup," Straw Hat said. "I always wondered why there were so many stories about beautiful women who lived at the bottom of a lake."

"Or the ocean," Bucket Hat said. "Can't forget mermaids."

"Nope. Or the sirens, neither."

Greg didn't want to listen to either of these guys. All he wanted to do was stare at the sculpture of the woman. Well, that, and make the sculptor work faster. Greg couldn't wait to see what the rest of her was going to look like. If he was lucky, maybe the man would give her great big boobs.

"When do you think he'll be done?" Greg asked.

"Competition's over at four," Straw Hat said. "Guess we'll all just have to wait."

All?

Greg looked around himself. The beach was filling

up with men. Not little kids with buckets and pails and shovels, intent on making sandcastles and sculptures of their own, but full-grown men with no kids in tow. All standing there, just like Greg was, waiting for the sculptor to finish creating a woman out of sand.

A beautiful woman.

"You know... this is kinda creepy," Greg said.

"Great art usually is," Bucket Hat said. Then he laughed, but his laugh had an unsettled edge to it. "Had a teacher used to tell me that. She's probably dead by now. She was a mean old biddy."

A gust of wind off the lake brought a musty stink with it. Sylvia had mentioned once that it might be fun to go swimming in the lake, but Greg had said no and meant it. When the sunlight wasn't glinting off the little waves the wind chopped up and the water was calm, the lake looked rank. The water was murky green, the rocks near the shore covered with muck and slime and who knew what all else. Sylvia said the lake had fresh water pumped in from an underground aquifer, but Greg wasn't convinced. He thought he might consider going out on a paddle boat someday, but swim in this stuff? No freaking way.

He held his hand up to shade his eyes and took another look at the sand sculpture. She was still a beautiful woman. Her cheeks were still round, her lips still full, but her smile didn't seem as warm now, the hollows of her eyes not quite as kind.

"Anything bad ever happen out here?" Greg asked.

Straw Hat glanced at Greg, but it was a fleeting glance, like he didn't want to pull his gaze away from the sculpture. "You mean anyone ever drown in the lake?"

"Yeah."

"Not that I know of. The city's pretty strict about not letting people swim where there's no lifeguard."

Greg had seen a patrolman ride a bike around the perimeter of the lake, had even seen the man tell people to get out of the water in the areas where there was no lifeguard on duty. The guy couldn't be everywhere all the time, though, and people in general were pretty stupid about following rules meant to save their collective asses.

"What about before?" he asked.

"You mean when it was a quarry?" Straw Hat asked.

"Yeah."

Straw Hat shrugged. "Who knows? Don't people always die in quarries? Deep pit with a bit of water at the bottom. Somebody could jump off the edge, end up at the bottom, who'd ever know?"

Water at the bottom? That must have come from

the aquifer. Greg wondered if that's why the quarry shut down in the first place, because the bottom of the pit filled up with enough water naturally to make working the pit unprofitable. His own bosses were always complaining about the profit margin getting smaller and smaller. Greg had no idea how quarries worked, but he could imagine that water where it wasn't wanted would throw a monkey wrench in things.

"Why you asking?" Bucket Hat said.

Greg shook his head. "Just curious." Because if he admitted what he was really thinking, he'd have to admit to something he flat out didn't believe in.

His parents, now they were true believers. They had swallowed all sorts of bullshit, metaphorically speaking. Aliens. Karma. Auras and Tarot card readings and conspiracy theories. Reincarnation. Past life regression. His parents had bought into all sorts of stupid ideas even though they had no proof that any of it was real.

They'd embarrassed Greg deeply, especially his mother, so he'd grown up to be a very here and now kind of guy. Sure, he might play video games, but they were always spy stuff or sniper games. None of those fantasy games that were so big online.

No superheroes for him. No little green men. No other worlds.

And especially, no evil spirits. Things like that Did Not Exist.

Life was all about working just hard enough to get by, having a drink or two or three on the weekends, and getting laid as often as possible. That was it, and that was the way Greg liked it.

Another gust of wind blew off the water. This time it picked up the dry dust and trucked-in sand on the beach in little puffs that swept around everyone's feet. Greg shivered as one puff of wind-blown sand swirled around his legs. Damn if it didn't feel like the caress of phantom fingers.

He stared up at the sculpture's sandy face. This time, he thought he saw a glint of something in the shadows of her eyes.

Something unfriendly.

"When do you think she'll be done?" someone yelled from the growing crowd of men on the beach.

The sculptor turned around. Greg was shocked to see that it wasn't a man working on the sculpture after all, but a woman. She was wearing a man's long-sleeved plaid shirt, and her hair was cut short and in a man's style, but Greg could see the rounded shape of her breasts beneath the loose fabric.

"Give me an hour or so," she said. "We'll be done

then. You boys don't mind, do you?"

Cheers went up from the men on the beach. Even Straw Hat and Bucket Hat cheered. Greg felt the need to join in, but he hadn't cheered at anything since the last football game he'd gone to in high school.

"Who is she supposed to be?" he asked when the cheering died down.

Not that he really needed an answer. The sculptor's shoulders were stocky and she was thick-waisted, that's why Greg had initially thought she was a man, but her cheeks were round and she had the same full lips as the sculpture she was working on.

The sculptor seemed to study him as if she was trying to figure out what to say. "A good woman," she said finally.

Greg wanted to ask her how old she was when that good woman died. He wanted to ask if that good woman had died in the quarry, but he had a feeling he already knew the answer to that question. What he really wanted to know is what would happen at the end of the hour when the sculpture was finished.

He wasn't sure he wanted to be here to find out, yet he couldn't seem to tear himself away.

He was aware when Sylvia came down to the beach to ask him where her frozen yogurt went. He promised to get it for her when he was done, but he didn't look at her as he said it. He couldn't stop looking at the woman in the sand, a woman who was becoming more and more alive at the same time the world around Greg seemed to be fading away.

The live band started playing around the same time the sun went behind a cloud. A gust of wind blew in from the lake, and Straw Hat's hat blew off his bald head. The man bent down to get it, and a little puff of sand struck him in the face.

Straw Hat shuddered and then he straightened up, his hat still on the ground. The band was playing some beach music song from the fifties at an ear-splitting level, but Greg still heard Straw Hat mutter, "I think I'll go for a swim."

Little bits of sand were stuck to the man's sweaty face. His eyes were distant and vacant, no longer looking at the sculpture of the woman, but at something only he could see.

Instead of turning around to walk back to the part of the lake Greg thought of as the kiddie pool, Straw Hat walked past the sculpture toward a sloping concrete ramp that served as a boat launch for people who didn't rent dock space at the little marina on the far side of the lake. No lifeguard was on duty on this part of the lake.

"Hey, you're not supposed to swim out there," Greg called out to Straw Hat, but the man didn't act like he heard. He just kept walking, his stiff-legged gait taking him down the ramp and into the water.

And he kept on walking.

"Hey!" Greg yelled.

The water was up to Straw Hat's shoulders now, and nobody seemed to notice. They were all too busy staring at the sculpture.

"Hey!" Greg shouted.

The only one who looked at Greg was the sculptor. The smile on her face chilled him to his core.

She *knew*, damn her. She knew Straw Hat was going to drown himself, and she wasn't going to do a thing about it.

Greg was no hero, but he couldn't just stand by and let a man die.

The water would be over Straw Hat's head by the time Greg got there. Whether he believed in weird shit or not, there was only one thing Greg could do to try to stop this.

He launched himself at the sculpture.

Greg hit the hard-packed sand with a solid thud he felt in every bone in his body. The sand at the base of the sculpture didn't feel like sand anymore. It was as hard as the stones that edged the lake and as cold as the water. It shouldn't have been cold. The rest of the beach was burning hot. The sculpture should have scalded him, but it didn't.

Greg scrabbled up toward the sculpture's face even as the sculptor screamed and grabbed at him. She was surprisingly strong. Greg had never hit a woman, but he didn't hesitate to kick her when he felt her hand latch onto the waistband of his shorts and pull. His foot connected with her ribs, and she stopped screaming long enough for Greg to hear angry shouts from the other men on the beach.

The ones who weren't walking into the water just like Straw Hat had done.

When Greg reached the woman's face, the sand on her cheeks cut his fingers. The sand wasn't soft like powder now. It was as hard and sharp as pieces of broken glass. Her full lips had peeled back to reveal razor-sharp teeth. Something lived in the deep shadows of her eyes. Something cold and malevolent and very, very angry.

"We didn't do anything to you!" Greg shouted at the lady in the sand. "I'm sorry for whatever happened to you, but it wasn't us, you get it? It wasn't us!"

Images bombarded Greg's mind. Men, grabbing

and pulling and touching. Men, thrusting and drinking and laughing. Men, hitting and pushing and throwing. And then nothing but the deep, cold oblivion of the murky water at the bottom of the quarry and the unending ache of a mother's empty arms.

"It wasn't us," Greg said again.

His fingers were bleeding. He held on to the top of the sculpture's head with one hand, her sharp hair cutting into his palm, while he made a fist with his other hand. He rammed his fist into the dark socket of first one eye, then the other.

Something chewed at his knuckles. He wasn't sure if the screams he heard were his own or those of the dying thing that lived in the sculpture.

After he destroyed the second eye, the sculpture turned to mere sand. Greg felt himself sliding down the side of the slippery sculpture. His hands and arms destroyed the woman's face as he went.

With the image in the sculpture gone, the men on the beach came back to themselves. Greg heard shouts from the water's edge, then splashes as people dove into the water or tried to drag themselves out. He hoped that Straw Hat got himself out of the deep water before he drowned, but Greg was in no shape to go after him.

Sylvia turned out to be a wonder of crisis management. She corralled paramedics who took one look at Greg's hands and carted him off to the emergency room where doctors removed more bits of glass than Greg could count. A police officer questioned Greg and administered a field sobriety test, possibly looking to make a charge of drunk and disorderly stick, but Greg came out clean. No one could explain how Greg cut himself on a simple sand sculpture. He figured that fact, if nothing else, kept the cops from charging him with any crime.

The city closed the lake to the public after that. Or at least they tried. Too many people had gotten used to taking walks around the perimeter, and the fishermen put up a stink at having nowhere in town to fish. The city settled for closing the peninsula where the sculptures had been.

Someone left a little cross on the beach one night, and the city didn't take it down. Only one man had drowned, and it hadn't been either Straw Hat or Bucket Hat. Greg felt relieved even though he hadn't really known either man. In fact, for all he knew, either of them could have been one of the men he'd seen in his head when he'd looked in the sculpture's eyes.

The next time they went to the lake, Greg was the one who suggested it. They didn't go for a walk. Instead they stood by the railing the overlooked the boat launch ramp. Somebody had left flowers next to the memorial cross.

"You're never going to tell me what happened, are you?" Sylvia asked.

"Nope," Greg said. He probably could. Sylvia was like his mom in some ways. She was open to possibilities. He just wasn't sure she'd see him in the same light if he told her the sand sculpture had been possessed by the mother of the woman creating it. A woman who'd been raped and beaten and thrown in the quarry where she'd been left to die by a bunch of men she never knew. Sylvia was becoming more important to him now. He was even coming around to the idea that she might be the one.

He put his arm around her shoulders. His hands were pretty much healed now, although they still ached at night like his bones were too cold.

"Aren't you weirded out being here?" Sylvia asked. "I mean, I am, and I didn't get hurt."

Greg shrugged. "It's okay. And the sun feels good."

Besides, he had to come here at least once just to see. He had a feeling he would know if that same malevolent spirit was still here, but he felt nothing but fresh, hot air and the occasional breeze off the water.

A mallard was swimming with her baby chicks out on the calm water, and he could see the vague outline of fish beneath the surface, lazy in the hot afternoon. Halfway across the lake, a couple in a paddle boat were making their slow way toward the eastern shore.

The flowers on the little cross at the base of the boat ramp wouldn't last long in the sun. The cross would last longer. Greg wondered how many people knew the cross was marking not one grave, but two.

Maybe that simple marker was enough, or maybe it was the fact that someone else knew now what had happened to her that finally let the lady of the lake find peace. Greg didn't want to consider that her peace came only when she killed a man who likely had never hurt anyone in his life. He especially didn't like to think about the fact that she could have killed him.

He squeezed Sylvia's shoulders. "How about we go get that frozen yogurt? I think I promised to get you some and I never did."

She smiled up at him. "You sure? I thought you didn't like it."

He shrugged. "I could learn," he said.

After all, he'd learned his parents had been right. The world was a lot bigger than he'd ever imagined. He wasn't sure how well he'd cope with that knowledge in the future, but for right now, he knew one thing.

Compared with battling a possessed sand sculpture three times his size, choking down a little frozen yogurt would be a piece of cake.

ONE SUN, NO WAITING

An old motel man like me, I appreciate good tenants. The ones who don't steal my towels, don't bust up the television or spill beer on the bed, who don't burn holes in the carpet and don't forget to turn the lights off when they leave—they're welcome at The Forty Winks any time. I always have room for 'em.

Better make it soon, though. I'm hoping differently, but I don't expect I'll be around much longer. I don't expect many of us will be around.

See, as it turns out, celestial bodies have tenants too. Who would have thought the sun was hollow and something lived inside? Sounds like a bunch of hooey, don't it? I might have said the same thing just a couple months ago, but these days it's pretty damn real.

Scientists concocted a fancy-pants name for it, but as far as I'm concerned all it means is that the sun turned out to be just temporary living space for folks on their way to someplace else, just like my motel. The last tenants in our neck of the universe pulled a damn good trick on us. Turned out the lights when they left. Just switched the sun off, like it was the Lord's own light bulb.

The good news—if there is any—is that the sun's on a dimmer switch. Scientists have a fancy-pants explanation for that, too, but I don't care much about scientific stuff. All it means to me is that the sun loses a little more light every day until pretty soon I guess there won't be any light left at all.

Right now my watch says it's eleven in the morning, but outside it looks like it's twilight. I used to think twilight was the prettiest time of day here in the Nevada desert. Everything painted a cool lavender-blue, the heat of the day just starting to bleed off into the night air, the sharp tang of sagebrush and the dry dirt smell of dusty sand tickling my nose.

It's not so pretty when it's twilight all the time, not when you know pretty soon the night won't ever go away.

"The damnedest thing, Jimmy," Maude tells me

every day. "Ain't it just the damnedest thing."

I suppose I should be grateful Maude's still here, still cleaning rooms and changing beds. A lot of people just took off, figured it was the end of the world and nothing much mattered anymore. Not Maude. She's worked for me for nearly twenty years. She's a good woman—not a looker, but she's sturdy and strong-bodied with gentle, faded-blue eyes and a quick smile. She puts up with my cigar smoke with only an occasional sour expression, and she has never once teased me about my receding hairline or my increasing waistline.

Folks used to say one day I'd marry Maude. Maybe I should have, but I guess I turned out not to be the marrying kind. Don't seem to me it matters much. We've been together longer than most people who walk down the aisle, and that should count for something.

"Ever wonder what we're still doing here?" I ask her.

Maude's hanging laundry out to dry. I rigged a clothesline for her in the little patch of fenced-in backyard out behind the motel office. We still have electricity, but brownouts are more frequent these days, so Maude decided to dry sheets the old-fashioned way, like her momma did.

I grab one end of a clean sheet and tack it up on the line with a clothespin. Maude fastens the other end, then adds a couple of clothespins in the middle.

"Where else should we be?" She nods her head toward the motel, a U-shaped building with twelve units, half of them full. "Like these fools? Running when there ain't no place to run to?" She snorts as she picks up another sheet.

"I heard a couple people say they were headed out to Yucca Mountain. Another one's going to the Lehman Caves. Going underground might not be such a bad idea."

It's already getting colder, even out here in the desert. When the sun goes out for good, I imagine it's gonna get seriously cold real fast. Being underground might be a little bit warmer.

"Like the government's going to let just anybody into Yucca Mountain. I don't hear anything about the President going to Yucca Mountain. That guy who ran against him—he's probably going to Yucca Mountain." Maude makes rude noise and takes a clothespin out of her jeans pocket. "You really want to live down there where they want to put all that nuclear waste?"

No, I don't. I never did trust the government's plan to bury the nation's nuclear garbage practically in my back yard. Seemed rude somehow, considering no one ever asked me how I felt about it.

"I heard the Lehman Caves have bats," Maude says. Maude don't like bats, calls 'em rats with wings.

Together Maude and I pin another sheet on the line.

"You don't seem altogether too upset about this," I say after a minute.

"Wouldn't do me any good if I was. Can't do anything about it." Maude shoots me a look. "You getting maudlin on me, Jimmy?"

Maybe I am, just a little bit, but I tell her no anyway.

Our conversation's interrupted by the sound of a car pulling off the highway. The Forty Winks sits seventy-five miles northeast of Las Vegas on a lonely stretch of State Route 93, a two-lane highway that don't see much traffic these days. The post office calls our stretch of road Greenville, Nevada, but the town's no more than a couple of double-wide trailers, a combination gas station/mini-mart, my motel, and a diner, the old-fashioned soda jerk kind with an eight-stool counter and three tables crowded against the front windows. Even with Las Vegas just an hour away, Greenville's businesses manage to make just enough money to stay open. People always seem to need someplace to stop, gas up, eat, or get a few hours of sleep.

My new tenant's a thirty-something man, looks like

a business executive, maybe a banker. Thin without being skinny, just a little shorter than my five foot ten. High forehead. Brown hair, thin on top; wire-rimmed glasses, not too thick. He's dressed in khaki pants, a nice golf shirt, and the gold watch on his wrist looks like it cost more than I made in the last six months.

Probably not a good idea to flash that watch around. It'd be a powerful temptation to some. So far most of the end of the world lawlessness has been confined to the cities. I keep my daddy's shotgun loaded and behind the counter, though, just in case. I expect that sooner or later I'm going to have to use it.

"I need a room," the man says. His eyes meet mine briefly, then slide away.

"Just you?"

"Myself and my son. He's five. He's out in the car."

The car parked in front of the office is an Audi, maybe a couple of years old. Could be silver, could be light blue. In this new twilight, it's hard to tell. The car's windows are tinted. I can't see inside.

"Okay," I say.

His eyes do the sliding away thing again. He's looking everywhere around the office. Everywhere but at me.

Under normal circumstances, this would set off my internal alarms. I've gotten pretty good at reading people over the years. Anybody who won't look me in the eyes makes me nervous. But hell, these aren't exactly normal times. Some people are dealing with it better than others.

I push a registration form across the counter along with a pen. "Fill this out," I say. "I'll need to see your driver's license."

He takes the pen and taps it against the form. "I... uh..." He licks his lips. "I don't have my license. My wallet was stolen."

"Then how do you expect to pay for your room? Got any cash on you?"

"I have some. I have my ATM card."

I shake my head. "ATM card won't work. Our machine went down yesterday."

I don't tell him that I couldn't get anyone to answer the phone when I called about the machine. I don't need television news to tell me that the system is breaking down. Not that I can get much on the television. I have a satellite dish hooked up to the motel roof—cable in every room here at The Forty Winks—but the satellites aren't broadcasting much anymore. About all I can get, even with the rabbit ears hooked up to my television, is KLAS out of Las Vegas, and that's too fuzzy to watch

ANNIE REED

for long.

Pretty soon I figure people will be down to bartering for what they want. But right now I still expect to be paid for my rooms.

"How much?" he asks.

I quote him a price ten bucks cheaper than my normal rate. Maude would say I'm too soft for my own good. But I never had any kids, and this guy's got a kid with him. I tell myself I'm doing it for his kid.

He counts out crumpled-up bills from his pocket.

"That's fine," I say. "Fill out the registration. You'll be in number 9, left side, in the back."

My new tenant turns out to be David Young of Henderson. I don't know what he's doing renting a motel room an hour and a half from his home, but it's not really my business. I hand him a key and watch him get back in his car and pull around in front of his room. Sure enough, a little boy gets out of the passenger seat. Kind of frail looking, dark hair like his dad, wearing shorts and a tee shirt. In this low light I can't see much more than that.

David unlocks the door to number 9 and he and his kid go inside. I watch for a little while longer, but David don't come back out to get any luggage from his car.

I hear Maude open the back door of the office and

66

walk over to where I'm standing by the window.

"Not being very subtle," she says.

"Nope."

"Got a reason?"

I shrug. "Nothing I can put my finger on. Something's not right."

Maude rests her head on my shoulder. "Lot of stuff's not right these days, Jimmy. Anything we need to worry about?"

"Don't think so." I put my arm around her shoulders. Maude always fit real well in the hollow under my arm.

"Got some rooms to clean," she says.

Yeah, and I need to fix the toilet in number 7.

Neither one of us moves away from the window for a long time.

I see the kid up close a couple hours later. He's sitting in front of number 9, playing in the parking lot next to his dad's Audi with a toy dump truck.

"Hey, son," I say, closing the door to number 7. The toilet's fixed now, just in case. There always seems to be someone who needs a room. Be prepared, my daddy used to say.

The little boy don't say anything. That's okay.

Kids these days get taught not to talk to strangers.

"You probably shouldn't be playing out here," I say. "Not the safest place."

He is a frail little thing even up close. His dark eyes seem too large in his face, his neck is skinny, and his little arms look like twigs sticking out of the sleeves of his green Incredible Hulk tee shirt. He's still not saying anything, and he keeps his eyes on that dump truck of his.

"You hear me, son? You can't play out here. Why don't you go back in your room and play there?"

"I can't," he says, his voice so soft I can barely hear it. "I have to play outside. Daddy said so."

"And why's that?"

He shrugs. He makes *vroom-vroom* sounds and drags the dump truck across the asphalt.

The shotgun blast takes me by surprise. The boy flinches but he don't look up. I about jump out of my skin.

It takes me a minute to realize the sound came from number 9.

My fingers are shaking when I open the door to number 9 with my passkey. The room has a nasty, metallic smell that's only partly gunpowder. The light in the bathroom's on, and the television's hissing static.

I have a good idea of what I'm going to find, but I'm still not prepared for the mess on the bed. David Young couldn't look me in the eye, but he had no problem staring at the business end of a shotgun.

My shotgun, I realize.

How he got it out of my office—how he knew it was even there—I'll never know.

I back out of the room and close the door. I feel like I'm gonna lose my lunch.

"Is Daddy done playing?" the little boy asks. "He said he wanted to play with your gun."

Yeah, your daddy played with my gun, all right.

I wipe the back of my hand across my face and swallow hard a few times against the bitter taste in my mouth.

"What's your name?" I ask the boy.

"Josh."

"Where's your mom, Josh?"

He drags the dump truck around some more.

"She went away. I wanted to go find her, but Daddy said she wasn't coming back."

I stare long and hard at the door to number 9, angrier than I've been in a long, long time. I can't understand how a man could do that to himself, knowing he's leaving his son alone.

After a few minutes, when I think I've pushed away most of my anger, I squat down next to Josh. My knees don't like it much, but I figure I need to be on the boy's level.

"Son, I need to tell you something that's not very happy."

He looks at me with those dark eyes of his. He's got a streak of dirt across one cheek. He rubs his nose with a dirty fist and leaves another smudge on his face.

"Your daddy had an accident when he was playing with my gun. See, grown-up guns aren't really toys, and your daddy should have—"

I stop myself. This boy don't need me telling him his daddy was a fool.

"Daddy hurt himself?"

"Yes, your daddy hurt himself real bad, the worst a person can. I'm sorry to have to tell you this, Josh, but your daddy died."

Josh isn't looking at me anymore. His eyes are focused on his dump truck and he's gone really still. "Like Fuzzy," he says.

"Fuzzy?"

"Our cat. She got hit by a car. Daddy told me she died and wasn't coming back. Daddy died and he's not coming back, just like Fuzzy."

He's quiet for a couple of minutes. I need to stand up or my knees are going to ache for days, but I don't want to move. I expected tears, not this eerie calm, and I'm at a loss as to what to do.

"What's going to happen to me?" Josh asks at last.

He looks at me then, and I can see he's sad, but more than anything, he's scared.

"I don't know," I say. "But we can figure it out together."

I stand up then, my knees creaking and popping. I hold out my hand to the boy and after a minute, he slips his small hand in mine. Together we walk back to the office. I'll tell Maude what happened and she can look after him. I need to make some phone calls.

I think it finally hits me how bad things are when it takes me four tries to get someone to answer the phone at the Sheriff's Office.

I recognize Linda Hopkins' voice. Over the years I've had to call the Sheriff on occasion, mostly to roust drunks who tear up their rooms. Linda's usually on dispatch when I call, and she's always crisp and professional. Today she sounds tired. Worn out.

"I got a problem," I say, and I tell her about David

Young and his son, Josh.

"I'll try to get someone out there, Jimmy," she says. "Don't know when it will be. A suicide's not high priority right now, we've got too many of them. Those of us left are having too many problems with the living."

I look outside the front windows of my office. I added an awning to the front of the office a few years ago. Maude went out and bought one of those fancy two-seater bench gliders and put it on the concrete sidewalk under the awning. She likes to sit out in the shade at the end of the day and read or just watch the world go by.

Now Maude's sitting on the glider with the boy, playing with some more of his toy trucks I found in his daddy's car. The sun's getting low in the west, and it's dark enough already that the lights in the parking lot have started to come on.

"What about the boy?" I ask Linda.

"I'll try to raise someone at Social Services, but I wouldn't hold your breath. People aren't going to work anymore, Jimmy. Be glad you're out there in the middle of nowhere. It's getting ugly here."

It's pretty ugly in number 9, I want to tell her, but I don't.

After I hang up the phone, I walk outside and light

up a cigar. Maude gives me a dirty look but keeps her thoughts on my smoking to herself. The tobacco finally starts to rid my mouth of the nasty taste I've had ever since I opened that door. I try not to think about what Maude and I will have to do if no one shows up to claim the body.

"Ain't coming, are they?" Maude asks, but it's really not a question.

"Sounds like they're pretty busy elsewhere."

"Figures." Maude ruffles Josh's hair, and I'm surprised when the boy smiles at her a little. "Guess we need to figure out what's for dinner."

We? "You staying tonight?"

I've got a little apartment behind the office, not much more than a rental room with a kitchenette. Maude has a trailer out behind the diner, but every now and then she stays with me.

"Thought I might." She grins at me, and right then I think Maude's probably the most beautiful woman in the world. "You like hotdogs, Josh? I think I saw a package in the freezer."

Josh nods yes. "Am I staying here?" he asks.

"For a little while," Maude says. "Just like me."

"Okay," Josh says.

He jumps down off the swing, taking his toy trucks

73

with him. I sit down next to Maude and wrap an arm around her shoulders.

"You trying to domesticate me, woman?" I ask her with a wink. With everything that's happened, it feels almost sacrilegious to be joking around, but at the same time, it feels pretty damn good.

"If I was trying to domesticate you, Jimmy Thompson, I'd tell you to put out that damn cigar."

I laugh a little at that, make a show of blowing smoke away from Maude before I stuff the cigar back in between my teeth.

"Star!" Josh says, drawing my attention away from Maude.

The boy's pointing east, and sure enough, there's a star hanging low on the horizon. The sun's not close to down yet, but I can see this star as clear as if it was the dead of night. I can see the moon, too, just a tiny sliver of dull red light peeking over the top of the mountain range to the east.

I shiver a little. Not too much time left in this old world. I hug Maude a little tighter.

"You know what I think, Jimmy?" Maude says.

I don't say anything, just frown at her. Maude never had much difficulty speaking what was on her mind, but I get a feeling from her tone that this is different.

"You've been running this motel for how long—twenty-five years?" she asks.

Ever since my daddy died in his sleep. "That's about right," I say.

"Out in the middle of nowhere, with Las Vegas just over the hill, all those glitzy hotels and fancy motels, but you still always have somebody out here who needs a room." She leans her head back on my arm and looks out at the sky, and we rock back and forth on the swing. "Now I don't know what's been living in the sun, or why they left, but I figure there have to be more of them out there. If nothing else, we sure know we're not alone in the universe. People always need a place to stay, and I'm guessing they do, too. And now we have a vacancy. Someone's bound to fill it. Might not happen in our lifetime, but then again it might."

I stare at her. In all the years I've known her, Maude's never been too philosophical. "You really believe that?"

"Of course! Don't you? Why else do you keep running this place, even now?"

That's true. I just never thought about it on a cosmic scale.

We sit there side by side on Maude's weathered swing and watch as more stars fill up the night sky. I wonder how many of them are just stars, and how many are homes to something that lives inside.

Maybe Maude's right, and I will live to see new tenants in our sun, see daylight so bright I have to squint against the glare.

It's a comforting thought.

I sit there and smoke my cigar, my arm around Maude, and watch Josh play with his toys. I find myself hoping that when the new tenants get here, they turn out to be good ones.

BAIT

Sarah saw the little girl first.

"Stop the truck! Oh, George, please stop the truck!"

George didn't want to stop. He was still too freaked by the run out of Reno. Half a tank of gas was all we managed to get at the last Arco station on 395 before the locals sniffed us out. Most of them don't come out into the sunlight, but every gas station in Nevada has a helpful tin roof over the pumps to keep the tourists from burning their tender scalps crispy red in the high altitude desert sun.

Not that Nevada has tourists anymore.

Not that anyplace does.

Doesn't matter that we're not from here. We're survivors, not tourists. Everyone else are locals, as George calls them.

George doesn't like to use the Z word. Sarah and I don't either. Makes it sound like we're in the middle of some low-rent horror movie. We're not. And calling them The Infected makes it sound like they've just got a bad case of the flu, no big deal. Trust me when I say, it's a Very Big Deal. End of the world, Big Deal. I keep expecting to see an avenging angel sweep down out of the sky, Hollywood blockbuster style, and rip us to shreds for fucking up God's grand plan.

Not that Sarah and George and I were responsible for this whole mess. We were never responsible for much of anything, which makes the whole last three people on earth thing kind of ironic, you know what I mean?

"George, stop the fucking truck!"

Sarah yanked on the wheel before George or I could stop her.

The truck swerved toward the shoulder of the four-lane highway. George managed to work the brakes to keep us from rolling into the ditch off the side of the road, but I got bounced around in the back seat. If I hadn't been wearing my seatbelt, I might have found myself thrown up front with my face kissing the dashboard.

We'd found the king-cab pickup a half block from where our last car ran out of gas. The keys were still in it, along with a gun under the front seat and a box of ammo in the glove box. Gotta love redneck cowboys. The guy who'd slapped an NRA *pry my cold dead fingers* bumper sticker on the back of the truck was nowhere to be found. I guess he was either dead meat or a shambling local. I pocketed his gun along with a bunch of the ammo. George drove, and Sarah rode shotgun. The arrangement had worked fine up till now.

"Sarah! What. The. Fuck?"

George looked like he wanted to slap her. He was a wiry little shit, black hair thinning on top. He wore wire rim glasses that never did stay up on his nose like they were supposed to, so he was always pushing them up. He had mean eyes behind those glasses, and thin lips that practically disappeared when his mouth pressed together in a tight, angry line.

He got mad at Sarah a lot, but she let him fuck her, and that must have counted for something because I never saw him hit her.

George was the one who wanted the truck—probably trying to make up for a lack of other equipment, not that I had any desire to ever find out. He made a move on me once, just once. I'd discouraged him—I'm good at that—and that had been before I got the gun. He never made a move on me again.

If he thought he could survive on his own, he'd probably dump me, but in this fucked up new world, there's strength in numbers. That's what makes the locals so deadly. There are just so damn many of them.

Sarah cringed away from George and turned scared eyes on me. "There's a girl out there, Holly. I saw her. Just a little girl!"

There were lots of little girls out there. Dead ones. Local ones, too. I'd never seen a little girl who was like us. Still human.

"Where?" I asked Sarah. "Show me where."

Sarah turned around and kneeled on her seat so she could look out the back window. "I saw her back there, in that field right off the road. Hiding behind the sign."

George hadn't taken us back on the interstate after we'd high-tailed it out of the gas station. Didn't matter anyway.

I used to catch a ride with friends sometimes, head east out of Roseville, take the freeway to Truckee and then turn off 80 for the drive up to Tahoe. We'd take the road around the lake, drinking and smoking, party up there on a beach in the summer or drive on down to Carson in the winter. Sometimes we'd head up through the valley north to Reno, where we'd stay with other friends until they kicked us out. I knew that the north-south freeway dumps into the old highway just south of Reno, then it's just a four-lane road that winds past old ranches divided up into acre lots with pastures for horses and cows and rural houses that look like somebody's idea of fine country living gone a little moldy around the edges.

We were about half-way through that part of the highway, on our way up to Lake Tahoe. We could have taken the more direct route that winds up the Mt. Rose summit, but George isn't as good a driver as he thinks he is. That road's two lanes of sharp turns and sharper drop offs, and we'd be fucked if a wreck blocked off any part of the road.

Sarah was pointing at an old wooden billboard off the side of the four-lane. The thing advertised a long-gone motel. The sign had been old and faded when I used to ride the party central line with my friends. Now it looked dead and creepy.

It was also the perfect size for somebody to hide behind to get out of the sun. An adult somebody, not just a little girl.

"Forget it," George said. "I ain't going back anywhere for some kid."

Sarah glared at him. George was stupid as shit. Sarah'd had a little girl. The kid had been with Sarah's ex for summer visitation when all hell broke loose. Somehow Sarah had managed to make it all the way to Sacramento on her own only to find her ex, or what was left of him, in the front room of his house, blood and brains on the wall behind him. The coward had blown his brains out.

Sarah didn't find her little girl, but I knew she never stopped looking. I wouldn't either, not if it had been my kid.

"Shut up, George," I said. "Back the truck up. Let her look."

He gave me a look in the rear view mirror that was supposed to scare me, but I don't scare easy. Not any-more. Not after what I've seen.

He slammed the gear shift into reverse. I thought he'd gun the engine, but all he did was let his foot off the brake. The truck rolled backward slowly. The fucker was conserving gas. Who'd have thought he had it in him?

He stopped when we were right in front of the sign. It was about twenty, thirty yards into the field. I never could get that measurement shit right. It wasn't like I had a rifle with a spotting scope, anyway. The handgun from the truck's former owner worked well enough, and I had an aluminum bat that worked even better.

I'm pretty tall, and I have wicked long arms for a woman. I swing hard, my aim's good, and what's more, I'm not afraid to swing. I got it in my head a long time ago that the infected aren't really human anymore. When it's them or me, I can pretty much always count on me.

George peered at the sign. "I don't see anything."

Of course, he didn't. Dry grass hid the entire bottom half of the sign. Whatever had been planted in the field had grown up tall without horses to keep it chomped down, and now it looked dry enough that a single spark might set the whole thing on fire. Welcome to summer in the desert.

None of the quasi-ranches on this road had actual ranch animals anymore. That was the real cosmic joke. Whatever bug or virus that had turned half the population into ravenous, shambling killers with dead eyes and open body sores had wiped out cows and horses along the way. People had spent so much time worrying about mad cow disease, it should have been the cows worrying about mad people disease instead.

The windows in the truck were dirty and dusty. Sarah rolled the passenger window down to get a better look.

I thought George might really hit her then. Open windows were dangerous. Hell, open anything was dangerous. That was another reason George liked the truck. It had air conditioning. He could drive with the windows rolled up and not die of heat stroke, and he could feel like a big man in a big truck, and he could feel safe.

"Relax," I told George. "I've got you covered." I took the gun out of my pocket to show him.

His expression said he'd like to take that gun away from me. Never mind that he had one of his own. In a contest to see who's better with a gun, I've got him beat and he knows it.

"There ain't nobody here," George said. "This is a fucking waste of time."

I didn't hear anyone through the open window, just the damn bugs. Cicadas have it made in this new world. They hide in the dry grass and the sagebrush and buzz the whole damn day away.

Bugs are going to be here long after George and Sarah and I are gone, long after the infected have wasted away to leathery flesh and brittle bones. I suppose I should be glad about that. Bugs are nature's own little garbage service. They'll neaten the place up nice for whatever takes over the planet the next go around.

Dinosaurs had their day, we had ours. I think I'd care more about what was coming next if I thought I'd be around to see it.

Sarah threw George a *fuck you* glare over her shoulder and lifted the latch on the passenger door. It made a loud clunk in the quiet afternoon.

Before I knew it, Sarah was out of the truck and walking toward the sign.

Not good. Not good at all.

George unbuckled his seat belt. "Damn Sarah's gonna get us all killed," he muttered.

I didn't want to get out of the truck out here in the middle of nowhere, not with all those nice, dark, empty ranch houses around where the locals could hide from the sun. They might not *like* to come out during the day, but if they smelled us, they might make an exception depending on how hungry they were.

But as much as I didn't want to get out of the truck, I didn't want George to get out either. I wanted him to stay right behind the wheel with the truck running so that if we needed to, we could make a quick getaway. Even if I had to dive into the bed of the truck while George was speeding off down the highway.

"Stay here," I told him. "I'll go get her."

I slid out from the back seat and into the bright

desert afternoon.

The place smelled dusty and dead. Sagebrush and dry grass assaulted my nose, and I almost sneezed. Gravel crunched beneath my boots as I took off down the shoulder toward Sarah.

The ditch that ran alongside the road was dry. Once upon a time the ranches must have used it for irrigation, but I'd be damned if I could see where the water had come from. I saw a couple of metal sheets pulled halfway up over concrete culverts set at regular intervals along the ditch. The rusty metal looked like guillotine blades stained with dried blood.

"Sarah, what the fuck?" I said as I caught up with her. "This isn't smart."

Sarah's dark eyes looked haunted. When I first met her, I couldn't peg her age. She could have been twenty-five or thirty-five. Her long hair was mousy brown with no grey, and her skin didn't have the saggy look some women get as they age, but her eyes were old. I learned later that she was twenty-nine. Her daughter had been six.

"I saw her." Sarah's voice was low, and she sounded like she had herself under control, but there was a manic intensity to her that I hadn't seen before. "I'm not crazy. She's somebody's daughter, and she's alone."

"How do you know that?"

She hadn't stopped walking, but at least she was slowing down.

"Nobody'd let their little girl be out here alone. Not anymore."

The world had always had crappy parents. I might have turned out differently if my mother had paid more attention to me than to her boyfriend *du jour*, but then again, maybe I wouldn't. Nature versus nurture at the end of the world. Not an argument I wanted to get into with Sarah while she was in bereft momma bear mode.

It was either protect Sarah from whatever might hurt her or go back to the truck and George.

Some choice.

I stayed with Sarah.

The sign was bigger than it looked from the road. Whatever whitewash had covered the wood once was long gone now. The boards beneath the old advertising slogan—from what I remembered, half-stoned as I'd always been back then, the motel had hawked itself as a place for a weary driver to pull in off the road for a few winks instead of falling asleep behind the wheel—were weathered gray and as dried out as the tall grass. Prickly blades of grass scratched at my hands and made me feel itchy. The sun was beating down on my head, and I could feel the sweat trickling between my breasts and down the back of my neck.

I kept the gun in my hand, my arm hanging down at my side. I had nothing to shoot at, so there was no reason to tire my arm by holding the gun in front of myself. Besides, I wanted to take in a wider view than I'd get staring down the barrel of the gun. Stupid, maybe—I'm not a quick draw—but guns are heavier than they look. I'm not a wuss, but I'm not a body-builder, either. If the back of my neck was sweaty, my hands would be, too. I didn't want to drop the damn gun in the tall grass just because my hand got tired and I quit gripping the gun tight enough.

When I finally saw the girl, I thought she was dead. Dead dead, not that virus/plague/wrath of God undead kind of dead most everyone who used to be a person was infected with these days.

She was just a little kid. She was hunched over next to the sign like she'd simply stopped walking, sat down in the grass, and died. Long, dark blonde hair matted with knots and bits of dried weeds hung down around her head, obscuring her face. She had on something that might have been a dress once but now was ripped and dirty and bleached almost colorless by the sun.

A small "oh" escaped Sarah's lips.

There was so much hurt in that sound it nearly broke through the shell I've carefully constructed around my own heart.

I hated Sarah for that. I'd earned my hard heart. It was mine, damn it. That impenetrable shell kept me safe and sane while I watched everyone I'd ever cared about die, including the ones I'd killed because they turned.

I'd need that shell in place if this little girl turned out to be somebody I had to kill, too.

I studied the sides of the little girl's body. Watched hard to see if she was breathing. The infected don't breathe. They only take in breath before they make that wretched moaning groan.

That sound still gives me nightmares. I used to wonder if they made that noise because somewhere inside their not-so-dead bodies was a trace of the person they used to be, only that person was trapped so deep inside the groan was the only call for help they could make.

I don't ask myself that anymore, not when I'm awake. My dreams do that for me.

The faded material covering the girl's ribs moved. Not much, and at first I thought I imagined it, until Sarah saw it, too.

"She's not one of them," Sarah said. "She's breathing."

"She could still be sick."

Sarah shook her head. "She's not one of them," she said again.

I decided to let it drop. This was her show. All I could do was try to keep things from getting out of control.

I stayed a few feet back from the sign. Nothing rustled in the grass around me. The only sounds I heard were the damn bugs buzzing in the sagebrush and the low idle of the truck on the highway.

"Hi, honey," Sarah said to the girl. "I'm not gonna hurt you."

Sarah leaned to the side, bending a little at the waist. She probably wanted to get closer to the girl's level, but that put her directly between me and the little girl.

"Sarah, get out of the way," I said.

She turned around and looked at me. "What?"

The little girl lifted her face.

Her mouth and chin were covered in dried blood.

"Jesus Christ!" I couldn't take a shot at the girl without hitting Sarah. "Sarah, move!"

I brought the gun up. Sarah, her eyes wide now, batted at my hand the same time the girl stood up and I heard the chains rattle.

Some sick fuck had chained that little girl to the post holding up one side of the sign.

I backed away, trying to put as much space between me and the girl as I could.

Sarah wasn't as quick.

I expected the little girl to lunge at Sarah. The infected moved slowly until they got a good whiff of a living person, then it was like they got a second wind or something. I'd seen them put on a burst of speed like a racehorse. That bit of speed let them catch you and kill you, even though in theory you should have been able to outrun something that was dead.

Instead of lunging, the little girl pushed Sarah. "Run!" she said.

Her voice sounded a thousand years old and as dry as sandpaper.

The door of the ranch house at the back of the field burst open. I heard something buzz past my ear like an angry bee a split second before I heard the crack of the rifle shot. I heard the second shot the same time Sarah made a soft little grunt and her body seemed to fold in on itself.

The third shot exploded out of the back of Sarah's head.

The little girl screamed.

I turned and ran.

I don't sleep much anymore. It's hard to sleep when you're afraid you might be the last sane person alive in the world.

Whenever I close my eyes, I see Sarah. Not when she got shot, not with blood and brains leaking out of her head—I've seen a lot of that—but how I imagine Sarah must have looked when the people who chained that little girl out by the highway as bait got done with her.

There's no reason for cannibalism. There's plenty of food left in the world.

I have no proof the guy with the rifle ate Sarah. It might not have even been a guy. The shooter's whole sick game might have been just for sport. I'll never know. I don't want to know.

George lost it when Sarah got shot. I guess he really cared about her. He tried to run the bastard with the rifle down with the truck.

The shooter was a damn good shot. I managed to get out of the way so George didn't run me down, but then a bullet smashed through the windshield and splattered his blood against the back window. I heard the engine gun, but I never stopped to see what happened to the truck.

I don't know why the shooter didn't nail me, too. Maybe two was a good day's haul and he didn't want the meat to spoil. I try not to think about what he feeds that little girl, but I saw her face. I'm pretty sure I know.

I ran down the highway until I couldn't run anymore, sure all the time that I'd feel a bullet punch through my chest before I ever heard the shot. I surprised myself by how much I didn't want that to happen. I always thought I was ready for the world to be over. Guess I'm not.

I thought I was tough, too. I'm not that either.

I found an abandoned car that still had some gas in the tank and no dead bodies inside about a half mile down the road. I wondered if the people that drove it this far had stopped because they saw a little girl off the side of the road.

I spent an hour trying to talk myself into going back to take care of the people who'd killed the only two friends I had left in this world. In the end, I told myself that my one little handgun was no match against a guy with a rifle who knew how to use it.

To make myself feel better about driving away, I promised Sarah and George as soon as I found something I could use to take out that farmhouse, I'd be back and blow the whole mess of them away.

It was a Rambo thought. I knew I'd never act on it.

I got to Tahoe two days later. I found some food along the way and managed to stay off the infected's radar. I don't know how long that will last. When I'm not dreaming about Sarah, I dream they find me while I'm sleeping, and I wake up just in time to see them reach for my eyes.

They like to eat the eyes first.

The lake's as beautiful as I remember it from my party girl days. Clear and crystal blue, surrounded by tall pines. You'd think at the end of the world, the water should be gray and filled with the ash of burned-out civilization, the mountains covered with the naked, brittle trunks of dead trees. The fact that this place is still pretty enough to take my breath away makes it all seem worse somehow.

See, I think I finally *got* it. Not the disease. The idea. I know in my gut that the world will get on just fine without us. Without me. Eventually the infected will die off when they have no one left to eat. It might take a generation or two, if there are enough uninfected people left for there to be a next generation of victims.

I haven't seen any sign of any other uninfected people at the lake. I haven't heard any sounds made by people, and sound travels well up here in the mountains. I've heard bears and coyotes, and one night, the howling of a wolf carried on the night breeze, but no cars or trucks or even a gunshot.

The house where I'm staying has a private pier. I walked down there the first night I got here, sat on the end of the pier and stared down into the water. The moon was a sliver overhead, and the water looked black beneath my dangling feet. It was cold, that water. It stays cold all year, even in the middle of a desert summer. Doesn't take long for hypothermia to set in, or so I was told all those years ago.

I was a coward for running away. Not from Sarah, she made her choice, but that little girl had no choice. She had no protector. Sarah would have protected her. Hell, Sarah gave her life trying to rescue that girl. Me? I ran away. I thought I was strong, but the guy with the rifle broke me.

When the infected find me, and I know they will eventually—Karma catches up with everyone, and I've got a whole lot of negatives weighing against me—I plan to take the coward's way out. I'll run down the pier and jump into that cold lake water. Swim out into the lake as far as my legs will take me, and then I'll just let myself drown.

Drowning's a painful way to die, I heard someone say once. It might have been on a TV show. I can't remember, not that it matters. I figure I can handle it. I'm already dying a little at a time every night when I can't sleep. The pain won't last forever, and I'll be able to look up through the water at the sky.

I just don't want to be eaten.

Please, God—if you're even there and listening anymore—I just don't want to be eaten.

NIGHT OF THE CRUISERS

Vince saw the first Cruiser on the way home after a grueling day flipping burgers at the DQ on West Fourth.

He didn't normally notice cars. He noticed the people *in* the cars, a longtime habit leftover from his former occupation. But cars? They were nothing more than a way to get from here to there that wasn't a truck.

Then again, Vince was a product of the city. Out here in the west, everybody had a car. Or a big-ass truck. In his old neighborhood back east, only the rich could afford to own a car. Working stiffs like Vince took the subway.

The only time he drove himself was when the boss sent Vince on a job and Vince had to steal some wheels to get the job done. The only criteria then was a big trunk.

P.T. Cruisers, now them Vince noticed. Little Tommy, one of JoJo's boys, used to say Cruisers were the yuppie version of an old-fashioned gangster car. Like Little Tommy would know what an old-fashioned gangster car looked like even if one came up and bit him on the ass. But you hang around a guy like Little Tommy long enough, some of what he said was bound to sink in. Vince had half expected Little Tommy to keep right on yammering about gangster cars even after Vince popped him one in the middle of his forehead.

Bullets tended to shut a guy's mouth up good. Vince should know. He'd popped so many guys over the years he'd lost count. Then one day the boss started looking at him funny, like the boss thought maybe Vince had run *his* mouth too much around the wrong people. Vince decided the wise thing to do was make a deal before someone popped him for knowing stuff he shouldn't.

He might not have made the deal if he'd known he'd be stuck behind a grill in a Dairy Queen in goddamn Reno eight hours a day. Some wiseass in the Witness Protection Program must have had a sick sense of humor, or maybe they were just tired of guys like Vince using the system to keep their own butts out of prison. Why else would they stick a shooter like him in Nevada?

At least it wasn't Vegas. He would have been made in Vegas within a week. In Reno it might take a month, six weeks tops. Vince had been flipping burgers at DQ going on five weeks. The only thing keeping his ass in place was knowing that no self-respecting wiseguy would walk around sucking on an ice cream cone that had a little curlicue on top, so Vince felt pretty safe.

Right up until the Cruisers started tailing him.

The first Cruiser made Vince think of Little Tommy. Vince felt bad about Little Tommy. Shooters weren't supposed to have feelings, and for the most part, Vince didn't. Little Tommy, though—the guy wasn't cunning or devious, he was just plain stupid. He let his mouth yammer on to the wrong guy, which got the wrong guy pissed off at the boss, and that was all it took. The boss didn't tolerate much, and he especially didn't tolerate guys who talked too much. The boss said get rid of the kid, so that's what Vince did.

Vince was waiting by the bus stop when the Cruiser rolled by. It was nothing much to look at. Dull silver paint job made the thing look like a fucking ghost in the desert twilight. He wouldn't have even noticed the car if it hadn't slowed down as it got close to him.

He was standing a few feet away from the bus stop because he wanted to smoke and some old biddy sitting on the bench waiting for the bus had given him the evil eye as soon as he took the pack of smokes out of his shirt pocket.

The wind blew every night in this damn town, and it kept licking at the flame of his lighter, threatening to blow it out. His hands smelled like hot grease when he brought the cupped flame to the end of his cigarette. The stench was in his hair and probably embedded in his skin. Even a long, hot shower couldn't do much about a smell like that. Vince should know. He'd dealt with worse, but not on a daily basis. Flipping burgers was enough to make a guy reconsider his career opportunities. Maybe he should just bug out, deal or no deal. The Feds weren't the only game in town. The sea was full of big fish who'd give an arm and a leg for the information Vince had locked away in his noggin.

Just about the time Vince was wondering if he should make a call to the boss's business competitors, the Cruiser showed up. The windows in the car were tinted so no one could see inside. Little Tommy's gangster-car bullshit popped into Vince's head as the Cruiser slowed down for no reason as it got close to where he stood.

Vince tensed up, half-expecting the passenger window to roll down just enough to let the barrel of a gun slide through. It'd be over fast. He'd see a muzzle flash, hear the soft *pock! pock! pock!* of bullets hitting his chest, and that would be it. He'd be done and gone and off to spend eternity with all the other wiseguys who'd been taken out by somebody a little higher up the food chain just doing a job.

When the Cruiser passed him by and sped up again, Vince actually let out a shaky breath.

Fucking Little Tommy. A car like that was nothing to get spooked over. Damn thing looked stupid, sitting low on the road like it was some badass piece of metal when all it was was a piece of crap little car like every other piece of crap little car pretending to be something better than it was.

Just like Vince, pretending to be someone he wasn't.

He crushed the butt of his cigarette beneath his heel. The old biddy on the bench had pulled out a cell phone and was laboriously typing in a message.

Vince shook his head. He would have guessed she didn't even know what a cell phone was. "Nobody's what they look like," he muttered under his breath.

He saw the second Cruiser from his window on the

bus ten minutes later. This Cruiser was cream-colored, the paint job a little shinier than the last. It had one of those flip top windows in the roof and a funny little hood ornament. The car probably cost the guy driving a couple thousand extra for those little doodads. If it was a guy driving. Vince couldn't tell. The windows were tinted on this one, too.

He turned away from the bus window and glanced across the aisle. The old biddy from the bus stop was staring back at him.

Something about her gaze gave Vince the creeps. The skin around her eyes was as wrinkled as the rest of her face, but instead of old-lady cloudy and washed out, her eyes were clear and dark. Her expression was neutral, but there was a coldness in her features that made Vince think of the old neighborhood women back east. The ones who'd seen their husbands and sons die in the streets, or whose husbands and sons had never come back from a long car ride to the boonies with somebody like Vince. Given half a chance, old women like that would jab a knife in your gut then turn around and cook dinner for the grandkids.

If he'd been back home, Vince would have asked this old biddy what she was looking at, but people out here didn't do that. "Don't stand out," Vince's handler had told him. Like a guy with Vince's accent didn't stand out like a sore thumb in a place like Reno. He couldn't control his accent, though he was working on it. The only thing he could control were his reactions. So Vince did what everyone else out here did—pretended not to notice. He turned his head back toward the window and looked outside. The moon was coming up over the mountain range to the east. Fat old moon. Harvest moon, he'd heard some customer say today.

Behind him, at the back of the bus, somebody belched long and loud, and somebody else giggled. There were a couple of kids back there, drunk or high, Vince didn't know or care. At least they were leaving everyone else on the bus alone. Vince hadn't had a serious confrontation since he'd been in Reno, and he wanted to keep it that way.

Another Cruiser passed the bus, this one electric blue. It didn't slow down as it passed Vince's window, but he got the impression someone behind the tinted windows had studied him.

He looked away, an odd sensation building in his gut.

The old biddy was still staring at him. Her hands were clenched tight on a white paper bag. Vince caught the edge of the DQ logo.

She must have seen him at work. Maybe she was trying to place his face.

"You like the food?" he asked her.

She didn't reply. Didn't move. Just kept staring at him with those cold, dark eyes.

For the first time in his life, he wanted a car of his own. Get out of this fucking town. Too bad flipping burgers didn't make him much more than what he needed to pay for his apartment.

Truth be told, that was what irked Vince the most. He'd had a sizeable stash of getaway cash back home. Every wiseguy did. It was just part of the plan when you worked a job with no pension, and retirement came at the end of a gun. The Feds made him turn over all the cash he had, then they gave him—*gave* him—just a little of his own money back to establish himself here. He'd paid cash for first, last, and the security deposit on his apartment, then bought himself some clothes since he'd had to leave his own stuff behind. He bought second-hand furniture and a used TV, but he didn't have enough left over to buy a car.

Vince seriously wanted another smoke but he couldn't light up on the bus. He yanked the buzzer for a stop a good half mile from where he lived. He half-expected the old biddy to get off the same place he did, she was eyeballing him so hard, but she stayed in her seat as the bus drove away.

Fucking imagination, playing tricks with him. That was all. Vince shook his head as he started walking toward his apartment. All that burger grease he'd been breathing must have congealed in his brain, making him paranoid.

Another P.T. Cruiser was stopped at the traffic light at the end of the block.

Maybe he wasn't so paranoid after all.

This Cruiser was deep maroon. The windows were tinted just like all the others. The wheels looked different though, like they were some kind of custom job that made the front end of the car dip down lower than it should. The headlights looked like prison spotlights, the grill like a smirking mouth filled with razor-sharp teeth.

When the light turned green, the Cruiser didn't move.

If Vince had been any other kind of a man, he might have turned tail and taken off running. He wasn't. He stood on the corner on the other side of street from the car and lit up a cigarette. Back in the life, he used to make men piss themselves with a stare like he gave the Cruiser, but the damn car didn't move.

When he finished taking a few drags on his smoke,

he made the shape of a gun with his right hand, his index finger pointing at the car, his thumb held up like a hammer. He brought his thumb down. "Pop," he said.

The car gunned its engine, a throatier growl than a sissy-ass Cruiser should have been able to make, then it drove away.

Vince smiled. Damn, he was good.

The half mile walk to his apartment helped sweat some of the grease stench out of his skin. He hadn't been walking enough. His belly was getting soft with the free meal he got every day as part of his wages. Back east, he used to walk everywhere. In this town no-body walked, and only losers rode the bus. Vince didn't like feeling like a loser. Funny thing, that was, for a guy who'd had no qualms ratting out the boss's right hand man.

The Feds had pushed Vince to rat out the boss himself, but even a guy like Little Tommy wouldn't have done something that stupid. If Vince had ratted out the boss, he'd already be dead, no matter where the Feds stashed him.

No, what Vince had done was pure genius. He'd ratted out a guy he hated. He'd had to implicate himself, too, but he'd refused to talk serious details until the Feds cut him a deal that gave him immunity for every hit he'd ever made.

Gus DeSenzo, the guy who'd given Vince instructions on who to kill—the asshole who thought he was better than every other guy on the fucking planet, including the boss—Gus was gonna fry, and Vince couldn't be happier.

Gus DeSenzo was a big fat slob of a man with little pig eyes and a blubbery Cupid's bow of a mouth that always had a little bit of whatever meal he'd eaten last caked in the corners. How DeSenzo had become the boss's go-to guy was beyond Vince.

Sure, Vince wasn't much to look at either. His eyes were too big and bug-eyed, his teeth uneven with a gap in the front, and his hair had never been all that thick to begin with. He couldn't grow a beard worth a damn, and the only place he ever put on weight was in his belly. He was what some people called "wiry," but most of the guys in the boss's outfit had called Vince a "scrawny old bastard."

Vince admitted he did look older than he was. Looked weaker than he really was, too. That's why even the guys who knew Vince was a shooter would still get in the car and go on that last ride with him. Everyone thought they could overpower him. They might have, too, but Vince was one quick, accurate shooter.

He never gave anybody a chance to take him out.

So as soon as the ink was dry on the deal Vince cut with the Feds, he told the guys with the badges and the fuck-with-us-and-you-die attitudes where the bodies were buried. Literally. He led them to his favorite dumping spots, and for each corpse the Feds dug up, Vince gave them a statement that not only identified the victim but fingered DeSenzo for ordering the hit.

By the time Vince was done, he figured the Feds probably had about twenty corpses on their hands and a gas chamber all warmed up and ready for Gus. It couldn't have happened to a nicer guy.

Vince lived in a cookie-cutter apartment in one of twenty cookie-cutter buildings constructed more than thirty years ago. The best thing he could say about where he lived was that it was anonymous. One damn building in the complex looked like the next, making it easy for anyone looking for him to get lost, especially considering that the buildings weren't numbered in any particular order.

The complex was looking well-worn these days. The paint on the walls was cracked and peeling, and weeds poked their sorry heads up from cracks in the asphalt parking lot. Every apartment had a numbered space beneath a covered carport. Vince's space had been empty since he'd moved in, and the weeds had pretty much taken over.

Tonight a P.T. Cruiser was parked in his space.

This one was sleek, black, and shiny. It looked like some big cat out hunting in the night, just waiting for its prey to show up. It sat idling, lights off, and Vince knew without looking that the windows would be tinted so he couldn't see inside.

He had a first floor apartment, but the place didn't have a back door. After he moved in, he'd worked on the bedroom window until it slid open without a sound, an emergency escape if he ever needed it. But the window was too high off the ground from outside for Vince to use it to get into his apartment.

He'd never thought he'd need his emergency exit to get in instead of out, and right now he did need to get inside. Vince never took his gun to work. It was in the bedroom beneath his mattress, out of sight in case he ever had a visitor with a badge.

"Fuck this," he muttered. The Cruiser was just a damn car. Probably some kid in the apartment building next door was throwing a party, and one of the stoners decided to park his ride in the nearest empty space available.

Vince walked down the sidewalk toward his apartment door like he owned the place. He glanced at the Cruiser out of the corner of his eye as he passed in front of it, half expecting the car to lurch up onto the sidewalk and come after him.

It didn't.

Vince was so busy telling himself he was being a dumbass that he almost didn't see the old biddy from the bus lurking in the shadows next to his apartment door. She was well hidden in the inky black shadows thrown by the set of concrete steps leading up to the second level.

What the hell?

There was no way she could have beaten him here.

Vince shook his head. Of course, she could. He'd gotten off the bus four stops sooner than he had to. All she had to do was stay on the bus and get off at his normal stop.

That didn't explain why she was here. Why she knew where to find him.

"Something I can do for you?" Vince asked.

She pointed at the name sewn over the pocket of his white uniform shirt. "Your name, it's not Eddie."

No shit, but no one here was supposed to know that. Vince still couldn't think of himself as Eddie. His name had been Vincent Servitto for thirty-eight years. He'd only been Eddie Franks for six months.

The woman had a faint East Coast accent, like she'd lived out here long enough to lose most of it in the desert heat and to flatten out the rest of her words like everyone did out here. Vince still had to make an effort not to sound too "back east" at work.

"You think you know that, huh?" Vince said. "You got me confused with somebody else, lady."

He pushed past her to his front door. She was as helpless as a kitten. She didn't even try to stop him.

"My Tommy, he told me about you," she said.

The name slapped at him.

Tommy. *Little* Tommy?

Was this old biddy his mother?

How the *hell* did she find him?

Vince made himself concentrate on opening his door. It wasn't easy. His hands were shaking. If she could find him, so could DeSenzo's guys.

"I told you, you got me confused with somebody else," he said.

The Cruiser's headlights came on, the beams switched to high.

Startled by the sudden light, Vince dropped his keys. They hit the concrete sidewalk with a flat sound, like a skull hitting cement.

The driver in the Cruiser gunned the engine, a sound far more angry and growly than it should have. Cruisers weren't muscle cars; their engines didn't make throaty rumbles.

Vince held up one hand to shield his eyes from the headlights. The lights were too bright, brighter than any headlights Vince had ever seen. The old biddy was muttering something now, something low and intense and in a language Vince couldn't understand. She'd moved closer to him while he was distracted by the car. He looked down for his keys and saw them peeking out from beneath her boot.

The old bat was trying to keep him from getting into his apartment.

Vince had no idea what was going on, but none of it was good. Had the Feds sold him out after all? Decided they didn't need his help bringing DeSenzo down? Or had DeSenzo flipped on the boss?

Gooseflesh crept up his arms. He needed his gun. It was the tool of his trade, not the damn apron and the overgrown pancake turner he used flipping burgers. He should never have left the apartment without it.

If he'd been a bigger man, he could have shouldered the cheap door to his apartment open. He wasn't, so he shouldered the old biddy aside instead.

She made a small "oh!" as she lost her balance. He bent over to grab his keys out from under her foot, and the light intensified.

Vince looked up in time to see three more Cruisers pull into the parking lot right next to the black Cruiser. All four gunned their engines, and the black Cruiser started to move.

It came up over the curb, only it didn't lurch up onto the sidewalk—it seemed to glide.

Vince fumbled with his key. The short hairs at the back of his neck stood on end, and his hands were shaking so badly he very nearly dropped his keys again. He knew the Cruiser couldn't get him—it was too wide to fit into the space between the apartment wall and the concrete steps leading to the second floor apartments—but logic didn't seem to matter. The creep driving the car just seemed to nudge it closer and closer to where Vince stood. The other Cruisers formed a phalanx behind the first.

"Some tough man you are," the old woman said. She'd fallen down, her flabby legs splayed out beneath her shapeless dress. "Tough man needs his gun to be tough. My Tommy, he told me about you."

"Your Tommy couldn't keep his mouth shut!" Vince jammed the key home and the doorknob finally turned. "He'd have been fine if he'd just kept his mouth shut."

The door opened. Vince started to walk through the doorway, headed for the safety of four walls and his gun, when something slammed the door back at him so hard the door jamb splintered when the door banged shut.

Vince pushed as hard as he could, but the door wouldn't budge.

He turned wide, unbelieving eyes on the old woman. She'd scuttled into the far corner of the landing close to the apartment door across from Vince's. Loud rap music was coming from his neighbor's apartment. He could scream his fool head off and his neighbors would never hear him.

"What the hell did you do?" he yelled at her. "What the hell is going on?"

The woman smiled at him. It was a horrible, evil smile that made Vince's balls shrivel.

"My Tommy," the woman said. "He's coming to give you a ride, tough man."

The engine noise from the Cruisers reverberated in the small space. Vince backed into the corner near his own apartment door. The Cruiser couldn't get him here. It wouldn't fit between the stairs and the apartment wall.

That didn't mean whatever was inside couldn't get him.

As if his thought made it happen, the Cruiser inched forward. Instead of running into the wall, the Cruiser seemed to collapse in on itself, squeezing into the small space like the car was made of liquid metal. It almost seemed to flow around the edge of the staircase.

The damn car was going to crush him!

Vince ran for the other side of the landing, but another Cruiser was squeezing in between the stairs and the wall of his neighbor's apartment. It was the cream-colored Cruiser Vince had seen from the bus. The one with the flip-top window in the roof.

As Vince watched, the window in the car's roof opened and Gus DeSenzo shoved his considerable bulk through the opening much like the car itself was squeezing into a place it shouldn't have fit. A line of blood, black as night, drew itself around Gus's throat.

Apparently the boss hadn't liked his second in command coming to the attention of the Feds. Even though impossible things were happening all around him, Vince had no trouble accepting the fact that Gus DeSenzo was dead.

"There he is!" DeSenzo said, his voice booming out into the night. "I been looking for you, kid. We all have."

The tint melted away from the black Cruiser's windshield. Little Tommy sat behind the wheel. The perfect hole that Vince had put in the middle of Tommy's forehead looked like Ash Wednesday ashes in the sullen light.

Little Tommy had finally gotten his own old-fashioned gangster car.

Behind the two Cruisers, Vince could see more P.T. Cruisers filling up the parking lot. DeSenzo had said "we all." Vince counted at least twenty cars. He knew who'd be driving each one.

"Why?" he said, his voice a harsh croak.

"Didn't think we'd let you out of the family that easy, did you?" DeSenzo said. His driver gunned the engine. DeSenzo's mean little pig eyes glared at Vince with a malevolent gleam. "Time to go."

Vince stared at the hood ornament on DeSenzo's Cruiser. He hadn't seen it clearly from the bus. He'd thought it was a greyhound or some other stupid shit meant to convey sleek speed. It wasn't. It was a gun.

But it was more than just that.

It was *his* gun, welded to the hood of a car that hadn't come off some assembly line, or at least not off any assembly line in Detroit.

Vince shot the old woman one last look. "For what

it's worth, I liked your son," he said. "I made it clean, one shot, so he wouldn't suffer. You remember that."

He never knew if she answered him. He walked over to the front of DeSenzo's car and put his hand on his gun. The barrel was tilted upward. He wasn't sure of the angle, but he thought it would be good enough.

The Cruiser's engine roared. Vince felt the power of it through the gun. He slid his finger through the trigger guard. It felt odd and backwards, but it would get the job done.

"Hey, DeSenzo," Vince said.

The fat man stared at him. "What?"

"You got pizza sauce on your mouth, you prick."

DeSenzo's face ballooned red with rage. Funny how a dead man could do that considering he had no blood left inside him.

Vince smiled. One small, final triumph. He was good with that.

He glanced over at Little Tommy. Tommy had made a gun with his forefinger and thumb. As Vince watched, Little Tommy let the hammer drop. Vince got the message.

It was time to go. No more Feds, no more deals, no more goddamn burgers. He wondered if he'd finally get his own car. What color would it be? He kind of liked the idea of candy-apple red. With racing stripes. If he had to drive a wannabe gangster car for all eternity, he hoped it was candy-apple red with racing stripes.

Vince locked eyes with DeSenzo. "This one's for you," he said. "You prick," and he squeezed the trigger.

He'd been wrong. The angle was perfect. The bullet made one neat little hole in the middle of Vince's forehead.

He'd always been one damn fine shot.

FOR A FEW LATTES MORE

The cowboy parked his horse in the handicap spot in front of Starbucks.

Terri almost dropped the Halloween coffee mug she'd just tagged with a second red clearance sticker. Ten minutes to closing. Of course. The strangest people always came in right before closing.

"You see that?" she asked Leon, who was sweeping the floor on the other side of the clearance display.

Leon craned his neck around a shelf full of travel mugs decorated with glow in the dark ghosts and goblins to look out the plate glass storefront. "Huh," he said. "That's a new one."

Terri watched as the cowboy in the battered hat and

leather duster got off his horse and wrapped the reins around the freebie community newspaper stand in front of the handicap spot. The cowboy was tall and thin and wore his hat low over his face. Thanks to the overhead lights in the strip mall parking lot, he was little more than a silhouette and totally out of place. Who in his right mind rode a horse in the middle of town?

"He's really going to leave his horse right there," Terri said.

"I'm not cleaning up after it," Leon said. "No way. Cleaning the bathrooms is bad enough."

He had a point. Picking up horse poo wasn't in either of their job descriptions.

Terri and Leon saw a lot in the way of weird walk through the doors of this particular Starbucks. Three blocks from the casinos, liquor stores, tattoo parlors and pawn shops of downtown Reno and a block away from the biggest dorm on the University of Nevada campus, it wasn't all that unusual to see frat pledges in penguin suits chilling in line next to bikers clad in black leather. Terri got propositioned by the frat boys on a weekly basis. The bikers went straight to offering Terri a free peek at tattoos on body parts she didn't want to think about, much less see. And that was on a slow night. Throw in a holiday, like Halloween or New Year's Eve or the anniversary of Elvis's death, and anything at all might walk through the door.

Like a cowboy straight out of one of the spaghetti westerns her dad used to watch when Terri was a kid.

"Just wait," Leon said. "He'll want a latte."

Terri shook her head. "Coffee, black."

"Quarter?" Leon asked. A quarter was their standard bet. They went as high as fifty cents when they were feeling lucky and flush.

"A dollar," Terri said.

Leon grinned. "You're on." He put the broom away and wiped off the nozzle on the steamer. Terri logged back on the register as the cowboy opened the door.

His boot heels clicked on the tile floor, and his spurs made jangling noises in time to his strides. He had something that looked like a small cigar shoved in one corner of his mouth. The tip glowed beneath the ash as he sucked in a breath. If the lit cigar wasn't bad enough—the front door clearly had a no smoking sign in not only English but the universal *You Can't Do That* symbol of a circle with a slash—more than just a whiff of the barnyard surrounded the cowboy like a toxic cloud.

When she was little, Terri used to crush over the

cowboys her dad watched on television. They all seemed so ruggedly handsome. Independent. Heroic. Whenever there was a damsel in distress—or an entire town in need of someone who could kick some serious ass—the lone cowboy would ride in and save the day. Clint Eastwood was her favorite. Back then, Terri never thought about what these guys must actually smell like. She was pretty sure she could have lived without knowing.

"I'm sorry, but you can't smoke in here," Terri told the cowboy when he stopped in front of her register.

Piercing blue eyes peered at her from beneath a dirty hat. "Coffee," he said around the cigar still clenched between his teeth. "Black."

Jeez. Dense much?

"Seriously," Terri said. "You can't smoke in here. We'll get fined."

Well, probably not, but she wasn't going to tell him that. Just because he looked like the crushes of her childhood, with his blue eyes and strong jaw and just enough stubble to be manly, not sloppy, didn't mean he could get away with smoking in her store. Even bikers didn't smoke in her store, and most of them looked like they could bench press a Harley.

Two freshman-age girls who'd camped out for the

last half hour on the easy chairs near the front windows, gossiping over their skinny mochas, took one look at the cowboy and giggled. He ignored them.

"Coffee. Black," he said again.

"Smoking. Not allowed," Terri said. "Please?"

He took the cigar out of his mouth and put it in the pocket of his duster.

Okay. That wouldn't have been her first choice, but at least he wasn't smoking anymore. Technically. She wasn't too sure about his duster.

"What size?" she asked.

He stared at her.

"Your coffee. Tall, grande, or venti?"

He still stared at her.

She pointed at the display of empty cups they used to show drink sizes. "Small, medium, or large."

"Medium," he said.

"Any particular blend? Tonight we have our house blend, Columbia Supremo, and Tanzania. Unless you want decaf."

He stared at her again. He was really taking this strong, silent thing a bit too far.

"How about we just go with the house blend," she said.

He didn't say no, so Terri called it good enough.

Starbucks was all about pleasing the customer, but she didn't think the training materials anticipated customers like this.

The cowboy paid for his coffee with dollar bills that definitely looked like they'd seen better days. Terri tried not to think about where that money might have been.

Leon had the coffee poured and the lid on the grande house blend before Terri finished making change. Leon wasn't just fast at making coffee. He also broke the land speed record for cleaning up. He had a theater major girlfriend waiting for him at home who made extra money as a cocktail waitress. A very shapely cocktail waitress, by all accounts. Leon was one motivated man.

The cowboy stuffed his change in another pocket of his duster. He headed back out the door but stopped just inside. At first Terri thought he might say something to the girls who'd giggled at him. Instead, he stared for a long minute at a blue flyer in the front window before he went out the door.

Most flyers posted in Terri's Starbucks advertised concerts at the events center on the north side of campus or poetry readings in the Fine Arts building. This particular blue flyer featured a picture of a smiling eighteen-year-old girl who'd disappeared after a party a few months ago. Initially the blue flyers had been posted everywhere on campus. Now only a few remained, which made a sad situation feel even sadder. It was like everyone had forgotten all about the missing girl. Everyone, apparently, except a weird guy who rode his horse to Starbucks for a late night coffee fix.

Terri watched through the front window as the cowboy fetched the cigar out of his pocket and stuck it back between his teeth. He hauled himself up on his horse and headed out of the parking lot.

Whoever he was, he was the real deal. A weirdo with a great costume and a rented—or stolen—horse couldn't have pulled that off without dumping his coffee in the parking lot. The cowboy looked like he hadn't spilled a drop.

Leon pressed a dollar bill in her hand. "Should have gone with the obvious."

Good advice. Maybe the cowboy was just that—a cowboy who preferred his horse to a Harley.

In a pig's eye.

The cowboy came back every night for a week, always ten minutes before closing, and always on horseback.

He wasn't Terri's most talkative customer, but he was rapidly becoming her steadiest. Every night he bought a grande coffee, black, and he always paid for it with rumpled dollar bills. Not that he called it a grande coffee. After the second night when they went through the same routine when it came time to figure out how much he coffee he wanted, Terri figured grande was his size and house blend his drink of choice. It fit.

At least he didn't smoke in the store anymore. As the week went on, Terri almost missed the cigar when the guy started to smell a little ripe. The cigar smelled a heck of a lot better than the cowboy did.

"Where are you staying?" she asked him on the seventh night, hoping it would lead to a conversation about nice warm showers and motel-provided soap.

"Manzanita."

"Hall?" she asked.

Manzanita Hall was the second largest dorm on campus. A few dorm residents were students in the undergraduate class Terri taught as a graduate teaching assistant. If this was just some prank to see how long she'd put up with a smelly cowboy customer, her students were going to be in for a whole different kind of lesson.

"Park," the cowboy said.

Manzanita Park was the green belt at the front of the campus. Thick with ponderosa pines and cedars and oaks, and, strangely enough, not a single manzanita bush, the park wrapped around a small lake that was home to a pair of cranky swans. The park had some pretty dense undergrowth here and there, but enough to hide a man and his horse?

Terri glanced at the bedroll on the back of his saddle. "You sleep in the park." She was pretty sure the campus had rules against that.

"Don't sleep much," he said. "Park's as good as anywhere else."

Except for the whole no shower thing.

"I hear the pond's good for swimming," she said. "That's what some of the frat boys tell me."

"Don't swim much," he said. "Not in winter."

Right. Because chilly water is too cold for a guy who sleeps outside in the winter.

She handed him his coffee, and he nodded at her from beneath his hat. It occurred to her that this had been the longest conversation they'd had.

"Nice talking to you," she said and gave him a smile.

He nodded again and touched the brim of his hat this time. His blue-eyed stare looked a little less severe.

"You like him," Leon said after the cowboy got on his horse and rode away, coffee in one hand, reins in the other.

"Do not," Terri said automatically.

"So if I smelled like that, you'd spend as much time talking to me?"

"I don't talk to you now."

"Liar," Leon said with a smile.

Just because she tried to be polite didn't mean she liked the guy. He was just strange enough to be intriguing. Like talking to a character out of a movie. Really. That was all.

The last customers of the night were two harried-looking girls with book-laden backpacks almost bigger than they were. Finals started in a couple of weeks. The undergrads in Terri's class were panicking already. Freshmen always panicked. Terri refused to freak about her own finals. She still had a week and a half to study. It just took a little discipline. And focus. And not spending too much time thinking about a mysterious cowboy who slept in the park.

"Have you heard?" one of the girls asked her. She was a semi-regular and someone Terri knew from around campus.

"Heard what?" Terri said as she rang up their order.

"Some guy tried to grab this girl after she got off the shuttle. Cops have the stadium parking lot all cordoned off. They've been there for hours."

"She got away," the other girl said. "So did the guy."

"Yeah, they announced it in class. We're all supposed to walk in pairs now. Or call the escort service to go to our cars."

"Like that's going to help. They don't have enough escorts, and how do we know it's not one of them doing this?"

"In the movies it's always the guy you don't suspect," the first girl said. "I bet it's one of the escorts." Her eyes grew wide. "Or maybe it's the shuttle driver. No one would suspect him."

"Too many witnesses," Terri said. "Unless you're the last person on the shuttle getting off at the last stop for the night."

Terri had said it as a joke. Sometimes she had a pretty odd sense of humor that seemed to work well with nervous freshman. Not tonight though. These two looked like they wanted to take notes.

Parking was a nightmare on campus. The university provided a shuttle service to the far flung parking lots at the north end of campus, nearly a half mile away from any actual classroom building. The shuttles were nothing more than half-size city buses and packed to overflowing during the day. Not great, but something. Except the shuttles stopped running at eight every night. Evening classes got out at eight-thirty. Seven o'clock classes didn't get out until ten, and by that time the classroom buildings were mostly deserted.

When the girl on the blue flyer first disappeared, Terri started carrying pepper spray in her bag. She still carried it, but mostly because she didn't clean out her bag too often.

"Look," she said, handing the two girls back their change. "Just be smart about it. Don't go walking around campus by yourself at night. You'll be fine."

She hoped they took notes on that.

An hour later Terri thought maybe she should have been the one taking notes.

"Just be smart," she said in an angry parody of her own voice with more than a hint of her mother's thrown in for good measure. "You'll be fine."

Right.

Driving through a construction zone on the way to work when you haven't checked the air in your spare tire in forever isn't smart.

She must have picked up a nail. Or ten. When she got back to her car after she and Leon locked up the store for the night, the right rear tire on her old Toyota was flat as a board. Leon was long gone by that time, headed home to his girlfriend and whatever they did that Terri didn't want to think about.

Terri had parked her car three blocks away in a service station lot. The service station closed at six. The guy who owned the place let her park there in exchange for tutoring his sixteen-year-old son so the kid could keep his grades high enough to play on his high school football team.

Okay. So she had a flat. No problem. She was a capable woman. If a guy could change a tire, so could she.

Unless the spare was also flat.

Terri stared at the dark and locked service station. Of course she'd have a flat at one of the few service stations in a 24/7 town that actually closed before midnight.

She could have called a tow service. Or a taxi. Or even Leon, since she had his number and he swore he never turned his cell off, even while his girlfriend was "entertaining" him. She could have done any one of those things—if she'd actually plugged her cell phone in the charger last night instead of burying herself in schoolwork until two in the morning before pouring herself into bed.

She looked around the outside of the station for a pay phone. The place was pretty dark, only a streetlight on the corner and the occasional headlights from a car driving by. She had to concentrate on her feet to keep from tripping on the uneven asphalt. Wouldn't that just be the perfect end to a perfect evening.

She found an empty half-booth, one of those things with two sides and a shelf for a phone book but no privacy for Superman to change clothes. The cord that used to hold a phone book ended in a ragged stump. A faded outline of a phone marred the formerly white wall, and the empty screw holes from where the phone had been stared at her like dead eyes. All very atmospheric in a creepy kind of way, but the one thing she really needed—a phone—was missing.

"Great," she said. "Just great."

Her voice scared her a little. It sounded small and frightened. She dug into her bag until her fingers wrapped around the canister of pepper spray. She was a modern, capable woman, fully able to handle life's little emergencies without falling apart.

She could go to her office on campus and call someone to tow her car. Except this was Thursday night, and no one in her department taught class on Thursday nights. Terri had a sneaking suspicion they scheduled it that way deliberately because no one taught classes on Friday nights either. After working the night shift at Starbucks for over a year, four nights off in a row was Terri's idea of heaven. The building would be locked up tight. While she had a key to her office, as a lowly teaching assistant/grad student, she didn't have a key to the building. Scratch that idea.

She couldn't go back to Starbucks. The place was locked, the security alarm set. The store manager was strict about not opening the place back up at night unless it was a matter of life and death. Terri didn't think a flat tire qualified. The other businesses in the strip mall were closed for the night, too.

She tried to remember if she'd seen a phone booth anywhere on campus besides the student union. She couldn't think of one. The new student union building was across campus on the far side of the stadium. Where police might still be investigating a crime scene.

And where, if she remembered right, there was a semi-enclosed and well-lit bus stop. She'd never taken the bus before, but even if she only rode the bus to city center, she'd be able to figure out how to get home from there.

Terri mapped the route in her head. She could walk around the outside of campus, staying on the sidewalks next to traffic. That would add about twenty minutes to her walk and involve a lot of climbing uphill. This was November in Reno. Ice liked to masquerade as clear pavement. The last thing she needed was to fall and break an ankle, or even sprain her ankle, when she didn't have a working cell to call for help.

The faster route was through the center of campus. Less hills, more stairs that the university actually treated with deicer. More lights along the walkways. More chances to run into other people who weren't going to attack her. The police would have scared the guy away for the night, right? No criminal in his right mind would try to attack two women on the same campus in the same night. Besides, she had her trusty pepper spray.

Five minutes later as she rounded the shadowy corner of a building so covered in ivy it was hard to tell whether the exterior was brick or stone, it occurred to her that she'd never actually used her pepper spray. Did pepper spray have an expiration date?

The English building was on her right, the Engineering building dead ahead, and the School of

Mines, the oldest building on campus, off to the left across an expanse of lawn. Each building was surrounded by thick shrubs and tall trees, and way too many places for a determined person to hide.

Maybe this hadn't been such a good idea. She was cold and tired and annoyed with herself, and she hadn't seen another person during her entire walk. She'd feel better if she had her pepper spray in her hand.

Except now that she actually wanted it, she couldn't find it.

This was ridiculous. She'd just had the thing not that long ago, but she couldn't put her fingers on the little can. It was like her bag had eaten it.

Terri held her bag open and peered inside. The light along the walkways wasn't the best, but she thought she saw–

The blow caught her totally off guard. One minute she was looking inside her bag, and the next instant half a galaxy of stars seemed to explode on the inside of her eyelids. The world canted to the side, and she was falling.

Falling.

Terri barely got her hands out in front of herself in time to keep from planting her face on the concrete sidewalk. She still hit the ground hard, jarring her entire body and stealing her breath. Her bag skidded away from her, contents scattering into the bushes where her attacker must have been hiding. The can of pepper spray rolled across the concrete, out of reach.

She scrambled after it. She got to her knees before the guy hit her again. This blow struck her in the side of the ribs. New pain exploded through her entire body, and she collapsed on the ground. He hit her again.

Where was the cowboy when she needed him? If anyone needed rescuing at that minute, she was it, but the strong, silent cowboy was nowhere around.

She was in serious trouble. Terri knew it even as she wanted to deny it. Something like this couldn't happen to her. She'd been prepared, damn it.

Her attacker had been silent throughout the assault. She hadn't heard him come out from behind the bushes, and he hadn't made a sound, even a grunt, when he hit her. When he dropped on top of her and started grabbing at her jacket. She wanted to yell at him, ask him why her, but she couldn't draw in enough breath to whimper let alone scream.

Get to the spray. That's all she had to do. She could still see the can just inches away from her outstretched fingers. If she could reach that, everything would be all right. It had to be.

A new sound reached her, a rhythmic, muffled thumping. Her brains were so scrambled, it took her longer than it should have to realize the sound was hoof beats across grass.

The cowboy.

Just like in the movies, the hero was coming to rescue the damsel in distress. Finally!

Except now this damsel didn't need rescuing.

Terri closed her fingers around the can of pepper spray. The pressure on her back let up. She rolled over, catching a quick glimpse of the cowboy, leather coat billowing out around him, barreling across the wide expanse of lawn on the quad. Her attacker must have noticed the cowboy, too. He was sitting up, looking toward the quad. Terri took advantage of the distraction. She got her hands in front of her and pressed the button on top of the pepper spray can.

It wasn't the best aimed shot in the world. Terri's hands shook too badly to hold the can steady. Still, enough of the gas must have gotten in her attacker's face because he yelled and started clawing at his eyes even as he got off her and tried to run away from the cowboy.

The chase was short.

Terri stood up and stumbled away from the cloud of pepper spray about the same time the cowboy threw a lasso around her attacker and jerked him off his feet. By the time Terri had her heartbeat under control, the cowboy had the guy hogtied.

Just like in the movies.

Had the damsel in distress in those movies ever felt like throwing up after it was all over?

"You're safe now, miss," the cowboy said as he gave the rope wrapped around her attacker's hands a final tug.

Terri rubbed a shaking hand across her mouth. Her own personal hero—a guy who slept in a park. Who'd have thought?

Then he went and ruined it all a second later.

"Wouldn't be walking around anymore in the dark like this if I were you," he said. "Not good for girls to be wandering around by themselves at night."

The last thing she needed was a lecture, but the cowboy did try to rescue the damsel. Might as well be polite. "Thank you," she said.

He touched the brim of his hat and nodded at her.

She heard the first siren wail on the night air. Someone must have seen what happened and called it in.

The cowboy got on his horse. "You need a ride?" he asked.

Terri didn't even have to think about it before she

said no.

That was the trouble with heroes. In movie westerns, the lone cowboy who rode in to rescue the town or the damsel was always cool and collected, handsome and enigmatic. He rescued the damsel before the bad guy could lay a hand on her. At the end of the movie, the damsel always rode off with the cowboy into a nice sunset, and everyone looked like they just got out of a long, hot bath.

That wasn't reality.

Reality was smelly and dirty.

Reality was a hero who didn't get there on time, and when he did finally show up, he treated the poor damsel who'd been fighting for her life—and doing a pretty good job of it, if she did say so herself—like she didn't have a brain in her head, and couldn't protect herself even if she did. When all along he'd been the one who was so out of step with the world that he didn't even know how to order coffee or that he couldn't smoke in a restaurant, and on top of all that, he slept in a park. A park!

The last thing Terri was about to do was get behind the cowboy on his horse, where she'd have to smell him up close and personal. No, thank you.

The cowboy turned his horse and rode away. Terri

realized she didn't know his name. Good thing the guy on the ground had seen him too. Otherwise, the police might not believe Terri when she told them about the guy who'd hogtied her attacker.

As she waited for the cops to show up, she finally took a good look at the man who'd attacked her. She could just make out her attacker's face in the dim light from the walkways. Even with his eyes scrunched up and watering, and his face red and blotchy, she could tell he had the kind of features some guys have who never seem to age. He could have been in his twenties or his late thirties, a customer or someone she saw around campus or a total stranger. He was unremarkable and unmemorable, and the last person a woman would feel threatened by.

Forget carrying the pepper spray in her bag. A pocket would be good. A holster would be even better. Did they make holsters for pepper spray? She'd have to look that up.

She didn't want her picture to be on the next missing girl flyer around campus. She'd come close tonight, and she knew it. From now on, she'd really be prepared. You could never tell who might stop in at Starbucks for a latte ten minutes before closing.

A cowboy.

A frat boy in a penguin outfit.

Or a villain hiding behind a smooth baby face.

STRIKE TWO

Lenny Masterson knew better than to ply his trade with kids in groups, but sometimes life threw a curve ball so sweet it would have been criminal not to take a swing.

These kids, three girls barely legal enough for the round of drinks lined up on the casino bar in front of them, never spared Lenny a second glance as he brushed by behind them. Women usually didn't. Most men would mind being treated like that. They'd run out and spend a fortune on hair plugs and a personal trainer, but blending in was part of what made Lightfinger Lenny so good at what he did.

The other part? Practice.

Lenny'd lived in Las Vegas for a couple of years now. The place was thick with tourists and southern California transplants who walked around The Strip all googly-eyed, trying to take in the sights and sounds all at once. Most of them never gave a second thought to the scrawny guy who bumped into them by accident, especially not if Lenny gave them the glassy-eyed stare of a lifelong alcoholic on a serious bender. When he was working, Lenny drank only enough to put the smell of alcohol on his breath. He could fake the look of a true souse when he needed it. He'd spent years of his life drowning his sorrows in a bottle. All that practice had to come in handy sometime, right?

Thanks to the school of hard knocks, Lenny had two rules he never broke.

One: No working kids in packs.

A kid by herself, her attention on her cell phone, why not? Lenny would be long gone by the time she ended her call, and even longer gone by the time she noticed her wallet was missing. But groups of kids were dangerous. Gangs especially—nobody messed with the gangs that were taking over more and more territory outside The Strip. Those kids would pull a knife on you for no reason, much less if they caught someone like Lenny in a middle of a job. Lenny steered clear of any kid wearing gang colors or sporting a dead-eyed stare. Lenny knew his limits. He was no fighter. He'd cut his losses and turn tail if he had to in order to save his skin.

Rule number two grew out of rule number one: Steer way clear of anybody connected.

That meant stay away from anybody who was any-body who mattered to one of the guys in charge. The city fathers might want the tourists to believe that Vegas was all cleaned up these days and the wiseguys were all gone. But guys like Lenny who worked the shady side of The Strip knew that while the old-style wiseguys might be gone, they'd been replaced by guys who made the old-school mobsters look like Tinkerbelle.

The tall kid at the bar, the brunette, she had one of those designer bags that cost more than a week's rent at the no-tell motel Lenny currently called home. That particular brand of purse was Lenny's favorite, not for any esthetic value, but because the thing was basically one big, open bargain bin ripe for the picking.

The brunette never felt a thing when Lenny took the slim wallet from the bag hanging off her shoulder. She just kept right on chatting with her friends as he slipped the wallet in the outside pocket of his sports jacket and made his way out of the bar.

He was prepared to stumble a bit and mumble a

drunken apology for bumping into her if any of the girls had looked his way. He didn't have to. A casual stroll across the gaming floor took him out the side door of the casino and into the oppressive nighttime Vegas heat.

Once outside, Lenny let himself smile. Man, even if he had broken Rule Number One, that lift had been sweet. It was almost as good as the crack of the bat connecting with a nice floating curve ball, the solid *smack!* of a clean shot over the first baseman's head. A line drive single that a speedy runner could stretch into a double if the fielder had trouble getting the ball out of his glove.

Lenny hadn't been speedy enough—hadn't been good enough, period—for the big leagues, but he'd never forgotten what it felt like to hit a shot down the first base line.

He didn't let himself look through the wallet until he was alone in a men's room stall at the back of a tourist-trap food court just north of the MGM. The little billfold had less than a hundred bucks in cash. No surprise there. Everybody used ATM cards these days. She had one of those, along with a couple of credit cards, a driver's license, and a few gambler's club cards from local casinos.

Lenny stashed the cash in the toe of one shoe. He

started to stash the ATM and credit cards inside the sock on his other foot. He didn't deal in stolen credit cards, but he had a buddy he could sell them to. Right before he pulled his sock down to tuck the cards away, he glanced at the name—Amber; cutesy name—but when he read her last name, he froze.

No. Oh, no, no, no.

He did not just lift a wallet off Mario Galletti's kid.

Lenny was a dead man.

Mario Galletti was a blend of old-style wiseguy and new age corporate mogul. He was in his late sixties now, and some said in his second childhood. He'd divorced his first wife so he could marry into the family of his biggest competitor. When his father-in-law kicked the bucket, Mario found himself in control of casino holdings not only in Vegas but on the Jersey shore as well as the Middle East. Scuttlebutt said Mario was one of the few Vegas guys who could scare the crap out of the guys in Dubai.

Lenny knew Galletti'd had kids with his second wife, but he'd never seen them. At least not that he knew. The girl he'd lifted the wallet from was about the right age and she'd been in one of Galletti's casinos, which meant the name on her credit cards and driver's license couldn't be a coincidence.

His sweet little line drive had just soured into a foul ball. He'd have to ditch the wallet and the credit cards quick, and then hope to hell no one had spotted him at the bar. Small time as Lenny was, if Galletti's people started nosing around, started asking questions about pickpockets working The Strip, Lenny's contacts would give him up in a heartbeat.

Maybe he should think about leaving town. He could get a new start up in Reno. They even had a brand spanking new minor league ballpark. If things turned out good, maybe he could buy himself season tickets. Watch a real game again. Hear the crack of the bat live, instead of only in his memory.

Lenny wiped down the wallet with a paper towel from the men's room dispenser. He used soap and water to get off any oil that had been on his fingers. He washed off the credit cards the same way and slipped them back in their holders using a dry towel to keep his fingers off the clean cards. Then he held the wallet under the air blower in the hope that any stray hairs or fibers would be blown away.

You couldn't live in Las Vegas without knowing about *CSI*. Lenny had no idea if what he'd done would work if Galletti's people turned the wallet over to the cops, but it was the best he could do.

Before he left the men's room, he dropped the wallet in the trash bin. The cash he kept inside his shoe. The few twenties Lenny had stolen would be chump change to one of Galletti's kids.

Lenny usually spent his nights in any one of a number of sports bars in the casinos. He didn't bet, not beyond a nickel-and-dime wager every now and then, but for the cost of a cheap drink, he could sit and watch every major league game on the bank of televisions lining the sport bar walls.

He'd grown up listening to San Francisco Giants baseball on a tiny black transistor radio. Alone in his room, he would listen to the announcers and imagine what it would be like to stand on an honest-to-God baseball diamond in a big-league park. The ump would yell *Batter Up!* and then Lenny would get into his stance over the plate. Stare down the pitcher, some schmuk from a Midwest farm state who thought he could strike a powerhouse like Lenny out.

Little did he know. Lenny'd wait for the guy to wind up and fire one at the corner of the plate. Right before the ball dove into the catcher's mitt, Lenny would let go with a mighty swing, and the ball would sail away over the right field fence. Home run.

Lenny'd had a shot at playing pro ball, but it turned out the pitchers who smoked fastballs over the plate were far better than the cornpone pitcher of his childhood daydreams. Lenny struck out more often than he connected. His legs were too short and he ran too slow. While his heart was in the game, he got cut early from every farm team who'd given him a look. In the end, all Lenny could do was catch every game he could on TV.

Tonight Lenny didn't stop off at a sports bar. Instead he made a beeline back to his room. The cash in his shoe might not be much, but together with the small stash of bills he had hidden inside the lining of his duffel bag, he'd have enough for a bus ticket that would get him the hell out of Dodge.

Lenny heard the click of a lighter the moment he shut his motel room door behind himself.

He froze, hand still on the doorknob. Somehow Mario Galletti's men had found out who he was and where he lived, and they'd done it in the time it had taken Lenny to try to dispose of the evidence. Now they were here to kill him.

Game over, hot shot.

He caught the faint glow from the flickering flame

of the lighter in his peripheral vision, heard air sucking in as someone took a drag on a cigarette.

"This is a non-smoking room," he said, hoping for a touch of bravado. If he was going to die, at least maybe he could go out with a little class.

"Ask me if I care."

The voice was female. Surprised, Lenny turned around just as someone switched on the bedside lamp.

The three girls from the bar were in his room. Not a couple of Galletti tough guys, only the three girls, still in their designer duds.

Maybe he wasn't out of the game just yet.

Then he saw the gun.

One of the three was leaning against the bathroom door frame, a lit cigarette held between the fingers of her left hand. She held the gun in her right. While the muzzle wasn't exactly pointed at Lenny, it was close enough to get the job done if he decided to make a run for it.

The other two girls from the bar—Amber Galletti and her shorter, blonde friend—stood on either side of the girl with the gun. The blonde must have lit the cigarette. She pocketed a lighter, then stood leaning back against the wall, her arms crossed in front of her ample chest.

"That's him," the blonde said. "I told you I recognized him."

The blonde looked familiar in the way half the girls under twenty-five in Vegas looked familiar. Skinny. Big tits. Makeup and hair right out of one of them wannabe model shows on TV, but her face wasn't nearly as pretty as her friend Amber Galletti's. Lenny had no idea who she was.

"Look, you got me confused with somebody else," Lenny said. "I don't know you, and I got no clue why you're in here with a—" He gestured toward the gun. "That ain't a toy, is it? You should be careful handling something like that. Somebody could get hurt."

Yeah. Like him.

The girl with the gun took another drag on her cigarette. "Is this the guy, Ms. Galletti?"

"Yes." The single word came out clipped. Angry.

"Heather?" the girl with the gun asked.

"I told you," the blonde said. "That's him."

Lenny began to get it. *Ms. Galletti.* The girl with the gun wasn't a friend. Amber and the blonde—Heather—were friends, but the third girl didn't quite fit in. Pleasant face, but not beautiful. Athletic build, but not fashion-model skinny.

The kid with the gun, she was on the payroll. A

bodyguard. Hired to follow Galletti's youngest daughter around but not be obvious about it. She blended in, just like Lenny did. Someone like her, she was just as easy to overlook.

"You got the wrong guy," Lenny said again. "I don't even know why you girls are here. I ain't got nothing worth stealing."

"That's a joke," Amber said. "Ha, ha. Very funny." She took two steps toward him, careful not to get in the way of her bodyguard with the gun. "Where's my wallet? Huh? What makes you think it's okay to steal from people like me and Heather? Huh?"

Had he lifted something from the blonde, too? He could have. He didn't remember every job he did, especially not if he celebrated with a few too many drinks afterward.

"I didn't do nothing, I told—"

"Shut up," the bodyguard said. "We watched the security tape as soon as Ms. Galletti realized her wallet was missing. Heather recognized you. She saw you on the monorail the same day she lost *her* wallet. That's two for two."

Now Lenny did remember. He never even rode the damn monorail except when it rained, and it had been raining up a storm that day. The big-chested blonde had been chatting on her cell, the tourists all around her had been *ooing* and *aahing* over the lightning like they'd never seen it before, and Lenny'd seen an opportunity. He'd taken it.

"Daddy doesn't believe in coincidences," Amber said. "I don't either."

Lenny swallowed hard at the mention of her father. "How'd you find me?"

"When someone named Galletti asks a question about where a lowlife like you can be found, people tend to answer," the bodyguard said.

A significant glance passed between Amber and the bodyguard, and Amber smiled. Lenny could imagine a hyena smiling like that—right before it ripped your face off. It looked like Amber had inherited more from her daddy than just his last name.

"So tell me where you ditched my wallet," Amber said, "and I might let you walk out of here."

Lenny knew he could make a run for it, but he'd never been fast on his feet. The bodyguard would shoot him in the back before he even got one foot out of the room.

"Trash bin in the men's room at the food court north of the MGM," he said. "Cards are still in the wallet."

"What about the cash?" the bodyguard asked.

"In my shoe."

Amber made a face.

"Keep it," the bodyguard said.

The blonde dropped her arms away from her chest. "What about me? Where's my stuff?"

Lenny shrugged, defeated. "Doll, I barely remember you. I can't tell you what I did with it. Probably spent the cash and threw the rest away."

She huffed at him. "You're just like the rest of them. Everybody remembers Amber. Me, I'm just part of the noise."

Amber turned her hyena smile on her friend. "Why else do you think I keep you around? We have the perfect relationship. We both use each other. You make me look good, and I get you in places your own family never could. So, Heather? Just shut the fuck up about your stupid junk."

The blonde shut her mouth, but the look on her face said she wouldn't hesitate to stab her good friend Amber in the back if she ever got the chance.

"Ms. Galletti," the bodyguard said. "I can make a call, have the driver go look for your wallet. He'll keep it quiet if I ask him."

Wait a minute. Keep it quiet? That must mean the girls were here taking care of business themselves because for some reason Amber didn't want her daddy to know about this little mess. Maybe there was still a chance Lenny could get out in once piece.

"So we're good, then?" he said, looking at the bodyguard. "It was all just a misunderstanding on my part. If I'd have known who she was—"

Amber belted him in the face before Lenny knew what was happening. Unprepared for the blow, Lenny lost his balance and hit the floor flat on his back.

"You know now, you jerk," Amber said, her voice ice cold. "I'm Mario Galletti's daughter. When I'm in the room, you talk to me. You show me the proper respect."

Lenny couldn't make his eyes focus. Her fist had caught him right under the cheekbone. His ear on that side of his head was ringing, and the room seemed tilted out of whack. Amber had definitely inherited her daddy's temper, not to mention his right cross.

"I will," he said, holding up one hand as if to ward her off. "Just so you know, I'm leaving town. You won't ever see me again."

"Pitiful." The hard, pointed toe of her high heel caught him in the ribs once, twice, and Lenny folded up on himself, coughing. "I'm out of here. Heather? You coming?"

Lenny half expected Heather to kick him, too, on the way out of his room. She spit on him instead.

After the two girls left, the bodyguard walked over and shut the door. "I think you got off pretty easy," she said. "Mr. Galletti has a rather more unpleasant way of dealing with thieves."

Lenny rolled into a sitting position. His ribs hurt. He'd probably have a whole color pallet of bruises tomorrow, but he could take a breath without excruciating pain, so he didn't think anything was broken. He'd hurt himself worse colliding with a shortstop the only time he tried to stretch a single into a double.

"Galletti would kill me, right?" Lenny said.

"Oh, not directly, although you might bleed to death eventually. No, Mr. Galletti now uses a punishment inspired by his associates in the Middle East when they have to deal with thieves."

Lenny thought he'd been scared before, but that was when he thought Galletti would only kill him. Galletti wouldn't really cut off Lenny's hand, would he?

"You're not... you can't..." Lenny couldn't even get the words out. "That's barbaric."

"And messy, but you'd be surprised at how well it discourages a second offense." The bodyguard flipped the gun around, grabbing it by the barrel. "Tell me—

thief—are you right-handed or left-handed?"

Lenny hesitated.

"I'll do both if you don't tell me," she said.

It was just the two of them now, and she had the gun turned the wrong way. She thought he was beaten, that he'd given up without a fight. Lenny would have if Galletti had sent his goons, but this was just one girl.

Before he could talk himself out if it, Lenny lunged forward.

The bodyguard had been standing only a few feet in front of him. Lenny's head hit her solidly in the belly. He heard the breath whoosh out of her, then they both tumbled to the floor.

Her head smacked down hard on the cheap motel carpeting. Lenny hit her, a solid left to her jaw. He was no fighter, but he was desperate. His hands were his living. Better to bruise his knuckles in a fist fight than face whatever she planned on doing.

He punched her one more time, a hard right to the body. She crumpled in on herself much as Lenny had done. He pushed himself off her and ran for the door.

Lenny had his left hand on the doorknob when the bodyguard's long legs swept his feet out from under him. That same cheap motel carpeting came up and punched him in the face, and the bodyguard went to work on him.

It didn't take much. The bodyguard had moves that would give a Kung Fu star a hard time, and Lenny was no martial artist. Before he knew it, she had him face down on the floor, her knee digging into the middle of his back, and the cold muzzle of the gun pressed against the base of his neck.

"I like it when guys like you fight back," she said, sounding barely out of breath. "It makes doing something like this seem a little more sporting."

She grabbed his left hand. Her grip was like iron.

Lenny struggled, but in the end it made no difference.

She didn't even use the gun.

The clerk at the bus terminal asked Lenny what bus ran him over, then chuckled at his own poor joke. Lenny didn't laugh back.

His body was one big ball of agony. The pain pills the emergency room doctor had given him kept the throbbing in his left hand down to a dull roar. All Lenny wanted to do was grab a window seat on the bus and sleep all the way to Reno.

The bodyguard had broken every finger on his left

hand, the middle finger twice. Lenny had passed out after she'd snapped the second one.

The doctor had wanted to admit him overnight "just to be on the safe side," the guy had said, mentioning potential nerve damage. Lenny said no. His broken fingers were set. He wanted to be long gone in case Mario Galletti caught wind of what his little girl and her bodyguard had been up to and decided the lesson wasn't quite good enough.

At least the bodyguard hadn't smashed his fingers with the butt end of her gun. He'd have to lay low for a while until he got the use of his hand back, but broken bones healed better than shattered ones did. In the meantime, he'd get by.

In baseball terms, Lenny was a switch hitter. His ability to bat right or left handed was the thing that always got him noticed by scouts and gave him any kind of a shot with a major league farm team. Ever since he'd been a kid, he could use his right or left hand for most things except signing his name. He'd just gotten lazy the last few years, using his left for most everything. Now it looked like he was going to have a good six to eight weeks of practice using his right.

He still had his money, though. The girls hadn't bothered to search his room or they would have found his stash in the duffel bag. The money wasn't a fortune, but pickings had been pretty good until he'd run into Mario Galletti's crazy daughter. Lenny figured he had just enough money to tide him over until his hand healed.

He might even have a few bucks left over to buy himself a transistor radio at a secondhand store. He could listen to the Giants while he recuperated. His old team was doing pretty good this year.

Who knew, maybe this time they might even take the pennant.

A guy could dream, couldn't he?

LOVE AMONG THE LLAMAS

Yesterday morning, I got in my car at seven twenty-five, same as always.

I popped in a CD—*The Best of the Doobie Brothers* this time—and cranked up the volume to keep me awake, same as always.

I stopped by Starbucks for a grande decaf latte, same as always.

Took the freeway to where I-80 merges with Interstate 395, that grand old mess of looped inter-changes and exits Reno locals call the Spaghetti Bowl.

Same as always.

Only not quite.

Instead of veering right and taking the next off

ramp, a left at the light three blocks down, and a right two blocks over into the parking garage, I stayed in the left lane and kept on driving east on the interstate.

And just like that, I quit my job.

Crazy, huh? Maybe I always was crazy and nobody ever noticed.

I had plenty of time after that to think about what I was doing. Once you get past Sparks going east on I-80, there's a whole lot of nothing but empty road since all the early morning traffic's going the other way. All those cars carrying commuters to their jobs, and none of them was me.

My heart hammered in my chest there for a while, let me tell you. I almost turned around at the next two off ramps I passed. But what was I leaving behind, really? An almost-empty apartment. A barren love life. A dead-end job for someone who'd only notice me by my absence.

I giggled a little about that. I could just imagine my boss's face when I didn't show at eight. At five after, he'd be checking his watch. By ten after, he'd be growing frantic.

At eight-fifteen, my cell phone rang.

I threw the phone out my car window—I didn't have an iPhone, just some cheap thing I got at Walmart—

which only made me giggle harder.

Bye-bye old life, hello you wide new wonderful world full of possibilities, you.

Of course, this part of that wonderful new world of possibilities was more of the same old, same old. Dry, sagebrush filled, hot as hell in the summer and freezing cold in the winter.

Nevada was a desert state. I should know. I'd been born here. I used to think the place was ugly, what with all that dry dirt, but yesterday morning, with golden, early-in-the-day sunshine streaming through my windshield, the world just felt different. I didn't know where I was going, where I'd stop, or what I'd do tomorrow. I figured I'd just drive until I got tired, had to pee, or I ran across something interesting.

As it turned out, I stopped when all three things happened almost at once.

Although, to be fair—the llama was what really made me stop.

I'd seen horses up close. Cows, too, and even sheep, but I'd never been nose to nose—or nose to neck—with a llama. But there, on the outskirts of Hazen, Nevada, a town that was little more than a blip on the road, I saw the words "Lighting Llamas" engraved onto a huge, curving sign over a rutted gravel driveway.

I pulled off the road and stopped beneath the sign. I rolled my window down and tried to decide if I wanted to get out of the car. I mean, there was a llama *right there* in the pasture next to the sign. Big, brown eyes, long eyelashes, creamy ivory fur. All I had to do was get out of the car, but for some reason I couldn't make myself do it.

The cicadas in the sagebrush on the other side of the road were buzzing up a storm. The day was already hot with the promise of getting nothing but hotter, and here I was, heading south in a car whose air-conditioning was spotty at best. What in the world had I been thinking?

I'm not sure why I turned off I-80 at Fernley except I had some vague notion about driving to Las Vegas, but now that I'd actually stopped driving, the whole idea seemed insane.

It wasn't like I'd had any recent trauma, any life-changing event that made me want to chuck it all and start over. I had two credit cards to my name and just enough in my bank account to pay rent next month. I wasn't some heiress off on a wild adventure. I wasn't a secret witness skipping town. I was just a woman in her late twenties—okay, okay, twenty-nine, are you happy?—who was tired of her everyday life.

But had my everyday life been so bad? Maybe if I turned around and went home, called my boss and told him I'd overslept because I had a migraine, he wouldn't fire me.

Right. And there really is a Santa Claus, Virginia.

"I am so screwed," I said to no one in particular.

I about jumped out of my skin when someone answered me.

"Could be worse," a male voice said. "Doesn't look like you've got a flat, and your engine's still running. You ain't having a baby in there, are you?"

"No!"

Good lord, no. You have to have a boyfriend—or at least a man with a working organ and a willingness to use it—to have a baby.

I craned my head around and saw the owner of the voice standing near the back of my car. My heart quit pumping double time out of fear and started thumping for a whole new reason.

If I'd been a Hollywood casting director looking for the next Sam Elliott lookalike for the next big budget Western (do they still make Westerns anymore?), I could have stopped my search right then.

The guy was tall but not too tall, lanky but a strong-looking kind of lanky, with a craggy face that looked ruggedly handsome rather than old and worn out. He had on a cowboy hat (of course), but the hair beneath it was wavy brown shot through with the beginnings of what I imagined would be a full head of steel grey hair when he hit sixty. He had a thick moustache and his chin looked like he hadn't shaved in a couple of days. He had on a well-worn blue plaid shirt and faded jeans, and (of course, again) dusty cowboy boots.

"Well, that's good," he said, his smile digging deeper crags into his face. "I ain't never delivered a baby before. Not if it don't have four legs and a powerful long neck, at any rate."

He was talking about llamas. "Is this your place?" I asked. I wasn't sure if a place where a person raised llamas was called a ranch or a farm, and I didn't want to insult him.

He nodded at me. "That it is." I heard the *little lady* even though he didn't say it.

Good lord, the guy really was right out of Central Casting.

I frowned at him. "You're putting me on, right? Do you really talk that way, or is it just something the tourists expect?"

His eyes widened for a minute, then he looked at the

ground at his feet. I heard him chuckle.

"Okay," he said. "You got me."

I knew it! Sure, I didn't know how I knew it, but I did.

When he looked back up, he was still grinning, but he had color that didn't come from the sun in those rugged cheeks.

"Hope you don't hold it against me," he said. "But not a lot of people stop out here." He shrugged. "I'm hoping to make something out of this place someday. I'm still trying out the patter."

"No problem." After all, I was trying out a new life, too. Sort of. If I didn't chicken out and go running back to my old one.

The second of my reasons for stopping made a sudden appearance. I'd polished off my decaf latte before I hit the Fernley exit, and now I needed a bathroom. In a hurry.

"Hey, is there a place around here where I can use a restroom?" I asked. I hadn't seen a gas station or fast food place since Fernley. I really should have stopped there and taken care of things, but I wasn't exactly thinking straight.

"Nearest gas station is ten miles back toward town."

Ten miles. I didn't think I could make ten miles.

He must have seen the hesitation on my face.

"Or you could come up to the house," he said. "I promise I'm not a llama-raising serial killer."

"Sure you're not," I said. "Isn't that what all serial killers would say?"

"Except for Dexter. He'd admit it."

That he would. *Dexter* was one of my favorite—

"Hey, wait!" I said. "You watch *Dexter*?"

"Satellite dish," he said. "When you live out in the middle of nowhere, it helps to have cable. Or the equivalent."

Huh.

My bladder twinged.

Good grief. It was either the llama-rancher's bathroom or go pee behind a clump of sagebrush and hope I didn't run into a rattlesnake.

Why, again, had I thought driving across the Nevada desert in the middle of the day without any kind of provisions or plan or even a change of clothes was a good idea?

"Lead the way," I said.

It turned out the llama rancher had a dusty old pickup truck, no surprise, but his ranch house looked like any other suburban house I'd ever been in.

"It's pretty new," he said to me. "I've got a buddy who's a developer in Fernley. He was doing pretty good until the housing market went bust, so I hired him to build me a new place. What do you think?"

"I think I'm back in Reno," I said. But in an upscale neighborhood. The house had high ceilings and spacious rooms, tiled floors, and a magnificent view of the desert landscape out of floor-to-ceiling windows in the living room. Even the bathroom was upscale, with an open area shower instead of a walled-in stall or a dinky little tub.

And that was the guest bathroom.

I tried not to snoop too much while I used his bathroom. The place was surprisingly neat for a man's house. Not that all men were slobs, but I didn't think most men kept a scented candle on a holder in their guest bathroom.

I sighed. With my luck, he was either gay or married, and either option left me feeling more disappointed than I should have been. After all, I was just passing through, and the only reason I'd stopped was for the llamas, right?

Of which I'd only seen the one.

My Sam Elliott lookalike llama rancher was in the

living room when I got done.

"So where do you keep the rest of your llamas?" I asked. I'd followed his truck down a rutted dirt road nearly a half mile before I realized it was his driveway. The fields on both sides of the driveway had sheep in them, but no llamas that I could see.

"The rest?"

"The sign did say Lighting Llamas," I said. "Not Lightning Llama."

He nodded at me and grinned. "Got me there." He gestured toward the bank of windows. "There's another field out back, over that little rise. I have four llamas back there, a male and three females. This time next year I hope to have seven."

I tried to see a boundary fence and realized I couldn't. "How much land do you have here?"

"A little over eighty acres."

Wow.

"And you live here all alone?"

I'd peeked inside his medicine cabinet—I couldn't help myself—and there hadn't been anything feminine on the shelves. No eye shadow, no lipstick, no makeup of any kind. Not that that meant anything. I mean, it was the guest bathroom.

His grin turned into a full-out smile, the kind of

slow smile that said he knew I'd peeked and he wasn't upset about it.

"Yup," he said. "Hazen's not exactly a hot spot for meeting women, and I work too hard to make the drive into Fernley more than once or twice a month. The only reason I saw you down by the highway today was because I was riding the fence line, checking for breaks."

He was standing pretty close to me now, but I wasn't picking up any serial killer vibes. The vibes I was getting were all first-date nerves type of vibes. Not that I'd been on a first date in a long time, but I dimly remembered the feeling, and I was pretty sure this was it.

"You check the fence line in your truck? I thought ranchers rode a horse to do that."

He chuckled. He had a nice chuckle, I decided.

"You've seen too many movies," he said. "Truck's faster and I don't have to clean up after it."

"Good point."

He tilted his head a little to look at me like he was giving me a serious once-over. I couldn't quite read his expression yet, but I liked whatever expression it was I saw in his hazel eyes.

"You're not like any other woman I've ever met,"

he said finally.

"Because I like *Dexter*?"

"Nope." He drew just a little closer. "Because you stopped to see my llamas, and you haven't complained once about only seeing the one."

True. Of course, right about now llamas were the last thing on my mind.

The first thing on my mind was how nice he smelled, even though he'd been out in the heat in a battered old truck, and the next thing was how I'd been wrong all along when I thought he might be gay. Definitely not gay, not if the way he was studying my mouth was any indication.

As we stood there, I realized he wasn't going to make a move without a little effort on my part, so I leaned forward just the tiniest bit. I don't know where I got the courage or the knowledge. My love life has never been what you'd call exciting or even vaguely adventurous, but here I was, in a strange man's house out in the middle of the desert, and I wasn't the least bit concerned he'd go all serial killer on me.

Yes, I most definitely had gone crazy.

That thought was wiped out of my mind when he kissed me.

It wasn't a grand, passionate kiss that swept us both

off our feet, nor was it an electric zing kind of a kiss that left me breathless. No, it was a perfect gentlemanly kiss, just enough pressure of his lips to let me know I'd been kissed, and enough of a brush of his mustache to tickle. He didn't touch me except with his lips, and before I knew it, the kiss was over.

I opened my eyes and looked into his. "That was nice," I said.

He gave me an *aw, shucks* smile. "Yes, ma'am."

I felt like punching him in the shoulder—a friendly punch, mind you—but I held off as something occurred to me.

"What's your name?" I asked. I'd never kissed someone before whose name I didn't know.

"Chet," he said.

"Kate," I said, feeling like I should hold out my hand for a shake. I managed to control the urge. A stronger one was taking its place. An urge to carry on with the kissing, and carry on soon.

Chet backed away from me, and I felt a sharp twinge of disappointment. It disappeared when he reached up to tuck a strand of my hair behind my ear.

"So," he said. "How would you like to go meet the rest of my llamas?"

As a follow-up to a kiss, "meeting Mr. Right's

llamas" was definitely not part of the dating handbook. I didn't care. This day was all about doing things outside the norm.

"I'd love to," I said.

Chet's llamas were the coolest things I'd ever seen. I even got to pet them, although Chet warned me that llamas, just like camels, tended to spit. I supposed I was lucky. None of them did.

After we finished communing with the llamas, we drove back to the house and Chet fixed me lunch. He made ham and cheese on rye, which tasted like heaven considering it had been a while since my meager before-work granola bar and latte. We took our time eating, and I got to hear about how Chet had inherited the ranch from a great uncle.

"He was Basque," Chet said. "He'd had this sheep ranch going out here for something like forty years. Never made a lot of money, just enough to keep himself from going under. His wife died twenty years before he did. I used to come visit when I was little. I was the only one of the kids in my generation who did, so I guess that's why he left it to me."

"Did he have llamas, too?"

Chet shook his head. "That's something I brought in. I'd heard that llamas were good at keeping the coyotes away from sheep, so I bought a couple. Then I found out gelded males made the best watch llamas. Well, by then I had another little llama on the way, and I just couldn't bring myself to do that to the little bugger, so I decided to raise them instead. That's when I got the idea for naming the place 'Lightning Llamas,' but so far you're my first guest."

I ate the last bite of sandwich. "You're a wonderful host for a man who doesn't get much company."

He was looking at me like he had after we'd kissed. I reached across the corner of the dining room table and took his hand.

"So tell me, Kate. Where are you heading?"

I felt a little embarrassed by my early morning decision to chuck my life out the window and just drive, but he'd told me about his life, so I told him about my morning.

When I was done, his eyebrows were climbing his forehead, and he let out a low whistle.

"I'm impressed," he said.

"You are?"

"My friends thought I was nuts to give up what I had to move out here and raise sheep for a living."

"What were you doing before?"

He chuckled. "Selling copiers. Never did quite seem to fit. I'm guessing your life didn't fit you, either."

No, it didn't. "I think realizing I'd been going through the motions—the same exact motions—every day, day in and day out, finally did me in. I just couldn't do it one more day."

He looked down at where I still held his hand. "You didn't answer my question, though."

"I didn't?"

"Nope." He took a deep breath. "Where were you heading when you decided to stop here?"

"Originally? Vegas. But I'd just about talked myself into going back. I guess you could said I was at kind of a crossroads."

"Crossroads at the Lightning Llama. Sounds like the title for a bad Western."

"Or a bad romance," I said, then wished I hadn't when he gently took his hand away and stood up from the table.

"Well, I guess you better get a move on, then," he said. "Vegas is still a pretty good drive from here."

He took our dishes into the kitchen. I hesitated for a moment, then followed him.

"Did I do something wrong?" I asked.

He stood at the sink, rinsing the dishes off and not looking at me.

"I'm too old to do casual," he said. "You've got your whole life in front of you. Me, I'm making a second life for myself out here. It's not much, but I enjoy it. I want to keep on enjoying it after you leave, you understand?"

Oddly enough, I did.

In fact, the more I thought about it, I decided that was another reason I'd pointed my car east and just drove. I was tired of living in a place where I waited by the phone for my first dates to call back for a second, or where I ate take-out by myself, or watched television alone.

"You know," I said, walking over to the sink. "We both like *Dexter*. We both turned our backs on a life that wasn't working. And your llamas didn't spit at me. That's gotta mean something, right?"

He grinned and shook his head. "You're something else, you know?" He let the soapy water swirl down the drain and turned to face me. "You trying to tell me something?"

I grinned back. "I didn't have my heart set on Vegas. All I told myself was that I'd drive until I found something interesting or I had to pee." I didn't think I should tell him about the tired part. "I thought the llamas were the interesting thing, then I met you." I touched his shoulder. "Good romances have started with less."

"Merely good?"

This time I was the one who chuckled. "Okay, great. Great romances."

He leaned forward, and this time he kissed me like he meant it.

We went to bed after that, of course, where we did a great many things like we meant it.

Chet didn't ask me to stay. He didn't have to. We'd already settled that issue in the kitchen, and besides, his bed was about the most comfortable thing I'd ever slept in. It probably had something to do with the fact that he was in it.

The next morning I didn't have a Starbuck's decaf grande latte. I'm pretty sure there's not a Starbucks within thirty miles of Chet's ranch, and besides, Chet makes pretty good decaf himself.

I didn't listen to the Doobie Brothers in my car.

I did call my boss—my former boss—on Chet's cell

phone to let the man know I wasn't dead, I just wasn't coming back ever again. He told me not to bother, I was fired. I think we both hung up on each other. It seemed a fitting way to leave that job behind.

Chet told me I should go back and get my things, and that he'd be happy to do that with me. We're going to make the drive to Reno tomorrow.

Today I'm going with him while he finishes checking his fence line, then the rest of the day we're spending in bed. Chet says he's old and can't spend the entire day in bed with me because I'd probably kill him. I think he's being melodramatic. He's no slouch in the bedroom department, grey or no grey in his hair.

I never thought, in all my wildest dreams, that I'd end up on a llama ranch outside of Hazen, but it's a future I can see for myself now.

Most people would tell me to take it slow, but I've been taking it slow all my life. Doing the things everyone expected me to do for so long that I'd begun to expect that's all my life would ever be.

Why take it slow when you know what you're doing is right?

And why keeping doing stuff that you know is wrong just because that's what you've always done?

Yeah, I don't have any good answers to those

questions either, and the beauty of it is I don't need any. I found my happily ever after where I least expected it.

I do have one question, though.

What are we going to name the baby llamas?

And for more Annie Reed...

*The following is an excerpt from the
opening pages of*

A Death
in
Cumberland

a Jill Jordan mystery

CHAPTER ONE

Nora Corbitt parked her car at the very edge of the dirt parking lot at Founders Park. The lot was full, but at this time of night no one would see her back here so close to the street.

The two baseball diamonds on the far side of the lot were lit so bright it looked like the middle of the day over there, but the banks of lights were focused on the playing fields, and the parking lot didn't have any lights of its own. Where Nora stood next to her car, she was hidden by the long shadows thrown by the few spindly trees that separated the lot from the baseball fields, and that was just the way she liked it.

It seemed like everyone in Cumberland had turned

out for the city league tournament. Grown men playing softball like their lives depended on it.

She'd seen flyers for the tournament at the grocery store. Nora didn't like crowds, and she hated sports and the men who played them. She wouldn't have left her house at all except for the cat.

"I have this cat, it's a stray, but my dad won't let me keep it. Can you take it? I hear you do that, right? Take in cats?"

The voice on the phone that afternoon had been young. Nora didn't trust the young, and she hadn't answered right away.

"I'm afraid my dad will kill it. He doesn't like cats."

Nora had stroked the calico in her lap, a beautiful cat with only one eye. The cat was like her, a survivor. That's all Nora had ever wanted to do—help the cats survive.

"Yes," she'd said to the young voice. "I can take it."

They'd arranged to meet in the parking lot at Founders Park. "After the games start. My dad will be playing and he won't notice if I'm gone for a few minutes."

Nora didn't ask why the meeting had to be secret.

She'd lived in Cumberland long enough to know that people who lived in small towns had their secrets, just like the town itself had secrets. Nora was one of them.

A secret, or maybe just a past the town didn't want to remember.

That was fine with her. She didn't want to think about the past either, only unlike the town, she couldn't help it.

No one was waiting for her in the lot. She shouldn't have been surprised. Kids played pranks, and they seemed to play more than their fair share on her.

She shivered inside her jacket. She'd stood waiting by her car for too long. It was fall in Cumberland, and in northern Nevada the desert got cold after dark.

She should go home, let the calico climb on her lap again, and stroke the cat's pretty fur until they both fell asleep. The calico was the only cat Jeremiah let her keep in the house. It was too old now to do any damage to his furniture. Mostly it slept on Nora's bed. When she was home, it slept on her.

She opened her car door and was about to get inside when she heard a voice calling to her.

"Over here!"

The voice didn't sound as young in person. It came from the empty field on the other side of the parking lot.

Nora squinted but couldn't see anything in the gloom except dried-out cheatgrass, tall weeds, and a vague shape that looked like nothing more than a darker shadow.

"Bring the cat to me," she said, "or I'm leaving."

"I can't."

Nora stood by her car. The open door and the little dome light inside gave her a sense of security.

She could get in and lock the door before anyone came at her in the dark. She didn't want to go out in the field, not at night, not without a flashlight. Not alone, and she was always alone. Why hadn't she brought a flashlight?

"If you can't come get it, I'll just let it go out here. It'll be okay, right?"

"No! Don't do that."

Too many dogs lived in Cumberland, and their owners didn't keep them fenced in. Coyotes roamed the empty fields. She couldn't leave a cat out here. What if it had been someone's pet? What if it didn't know how to survive on its own?

"I'm coming," she said. "Just wait a minute."

Nora had a gun in her purse. She never traveled anywhere without it.

She got the gun and dropped it in the deep pocket of her jacket. She shut her car door but didn't lock it. She'd be able to run back to her car and lock herself inside if she needed to. Until then, she'd keep her hand on the gun in her pocket and everything would be fine.

Even after the gloom of the parking lot, the darkness of the field was nearly absolute. The ground beneath the tall, dry weeds was rocky and uneven.

If she just concentrated on putting one foot in front of the next, she would be all right. She'd take the cat and go back to her car. It would be scared, but she'd take care of it.

She could be strong for the cat. She was strong. She'd survived. She could do a simple thing like this. There was nothing to be frightened of. She had a gun. This time she had a gun.

The sharp *crack!* of a bat connecting solidly with a ball made her flinch. The crowd at the baseball field erupted in cheers.

The skin on Nora's neck crept up in gooseflesh. The night was too dark in this field, and she'd walked too far. She heard rustling in the field but she couldn't see the dark shape anymore. She needed to get back to her car.

"Bring me the cat," she said, dismayed but not surprised to hear the trembling in her voice.

"It's over here."

Now the voice was behind her.

How did it get behind her?

Nora whirled, dragging the gun out of her pocket.

Something solid connected with her hand just as she got a good grip on the gun.

The pain was enormous. Nora cried out as the gun went flying from her suddenly numb and useless fingers.

"You're so easy," the voice said, this time sounding not like a child at all.

She clutched her broken hand to her chest as her attacker laughed at her. The parking lot was on the far side of that laughter. She couldn't get there without being hit again.

She turned in the other direction and fled.

"That's right. Run!"

The uneven ground nearly made her stumble. Every stride sent electric, white-hot jolts of pain through her injured arm. She lost a shoe in the dead weeds, and a rock bit into the flesh at the bottom of her foot, but she would have kept running if her ribs hadn't suddenly exploded in pain.

The force of the blow knocked her off her feet. She landed on her broken hand, and this time the pain was so horrible she nearly blacked out. She tried to scream but she couldn't get enough air in her lungs.

"Get up," her attacker said.

"Please." The word was little more than a whimper forced out through a red haze of pain.

"Get up!"

Nora did.

She managed only a few more shaky strides before another blow sent her sprawling.

The next blow came down on the back of her head.

Dirt and dry grass clogged her nose and got into her open mouth. A buzzing, ringing noise filled her head. She sputtered, trying to spit out the dirt. She couldn't get her legs to work. She tried to pull herself forward with her good hand, but her fingers scrabbled uselessly at the ground.

One more blow landed on her head, and the buzzing got so loud it had blotted out everything else. The dark night had given way to a tunnel of black so thick Nora felt like she was drowning in tar.

For a moment she saw the calico's sweet, one-eyed face in that blackness, saw the faces of all the cats she had ever loved and cared for and lost, but then they faded, too, even as her fingers stopped moving and her breathing slowed.

By the time the next blow fell, Nora Corbitt was dead.

CHAPTER TWO

Cliff & Mattie's Diner faced Main Street, Cumberland's name for Highway 50 where the lonely two-lane desert highway widened to four lanes for the mile and a half it passed through town.

Sixty miles southeast of Reno, Cumberland was the only town to speak of in Silverado County, the third largest county in Nevada.

Cumberland was also the Silverado county seat, and the place Sheriff Jill Jordan called home, along with some forty-eight hundred other permanent residents, an ever-shifting population of transients who lived on the outskirts of town, and the occasional traveler who wanted a place to stop and gas up on the way to either Reno or Las Vegas.

Travelers usually bypassed Cliff & Mattie's in favor of the $3.99 all-you-can-eat buffet at the Golden Nugget Hotel & Casino, only a half-mile down Main from the diner.

Locals preferred the homey atmosphere of Cliff & Mattie's. Everybody who was a regular knew everyone else, and gossip was served right alongside simple meals in ample portions. If anything of importance happened in Cumberland, all the regulars knew about it before the local newspaper even caught a whiff.

Gossip was the reason Sheriff Jill Jordan ate breakfast at Cliff & Mattie's five days a week, just like her father had. Charlie Jordan had been a patrol deputy. He'd taught his daughter at a young age that in order to protect and serve the public, an officer needed to get to know the citizens that officer served.

In Cumberland most gossip had just a big enough kernel of truth in it to give Jill an opportunity to stop small problems before they became official complaints.

Back in the days when Jill's father ate breakfast at the diner, the red leatherette booths had been new and soft, the cushions on the aluminum-edged stools at the counter still had enough padding to be comfortable, the black enamel on the tables and chairs had been new and unchipped, and the black-and-white checkerboard linoleum floor was slick and shiny.

The red leatherette in the booths had stiffened and cracked in a few places over the years, and the cushions on the stools weren't quite as comfortable, but Cliff & Mattie's would always be the heart of Cumberland.

On this October morning Jill took her usual seat at the end of the counter where it curved toward the hallway leading to the restrooms. The spot let her see the rest of the diner while she ate. It was also isolated enough to let her read the morning paper in peace if she wanted.

"Morning, Jill." Tina Williams, the morning waitress, set a small silver pot of hot water next to Jill's coffee cup. A bag of decaf Earl Grey tea lay on the white paper doily that decorated the saucer beneath the teapot. "Same as usual?"

Jill put down her paper next to the place setting. "Yeah, thanks." She dipped the teabag in the hot water. Decaf Earl Grey wasn't coffee, but her doctor said it was better for Jill's blood pressure.

Tina was a divorced mom like Jill, but ten years younger. Tina had a good figure and what Jill thought of as Loretta Lynn hair—medium brunette, long and cut in layers that Tina styled in large, bouncy curls. Her face was pleasant in a plain kind of way, but the plain disappeared when Tina smiled. That's when Tina resembled her daughter Charlotte the most. Tina must have been beautiful when she was Charlotte's age, before life drained the pretty from her features.

Charlotte was Jill's daughter's best friend. Jill had met Charlotte when both girls were nine. Charlotte had ridden the bus home from school one afternoon with Emily. Charlotte had announced to a surprised Jill that she was an accident that wasn't supposed to happen, but that was okay because her mom loved her even if her daddy didn't.

Charlotte's bluntness hadn't dimmed as she grew older. In a way, Jill found it refreshing, but sometimes she wondered how Tina put up with it on a constant basis.

"The girls get up okay this morning?" Jill asked. Emily had spent the night at Charlotte's, giving Jill an unaccustomed quiet morning at home by herself with no music blaring from Emily's room.

Tina chuckled. "You should have heard them. All excited about Homecoming. Making plans to go to the bonfire Friday night, even talking about going to the game on Saturday before the dance. You letting Emily go to that?"

Jill nodded. "It's all part of the high school experience."

Emily and Charlotte were high school freshmen. By the time they got to be seniors, they might be too jaded to go to any Homecoming events—unless they were dating football players—but as freshmen, high school was still new and fresh and exciting.

"Don't the seniors have beer at the bonfire?" Tina asked. "I mean, they did back when I was in high school. Or... what I remember of high school anyway."

Jill had done the math a long time ago. Given her age, Tina must have dropped out of high school before her senior year to have her daughter. Back in those days, pregnant students weren't allowed in the state's public schools.

Tina never said if she finished high school after Charlotte was born, and Jill didn't ask. She was one of the few people in Cumberland who knew that the boy who'd gotten Tina pregnant and then deserted her had robbed a convenience store in Reno a few months later and shot the clerk.

Last year he'd come back to Cumberland to get to know his daughter, he'd said. Jill had kept a close watch on him. So far he'd been a model citizen. Maybe he'd learned his lesson doing time at the state prison in Carson City. Jill hoped so.

"I'll have an officer or two on site at the school," Jill said. "There won't be any beer."

She had assigned an officer to patrol the bonfire every year since she'd taken office. The kids grumbled about it, and she'd even had a call from the football coach the first year. He hadn't come right out and said his boys resented not being able to drink at the bonfire, a long-standing tradition among the seniors, but the implication was clear.

Jill didn't care. Minors didn't drink in Silverado County if she could help it. Teenagers and alcohol didn't mix. Not that adults were much better, but at least she could do something about the kids. It made her vastly uncool among the high school kids, according to Emily. Jill didn't much care about that either.

Tina breathed a sigh of relief. "Good. Makes me feel a little better about letting Charlotte go. Don't want her making my mistakes, you know?" She scribbled something on her order pad, presumably Jill's normal breakfast order. "Be back with your meal in a few."

Jill poured herself a cup of tea and opened the morning edition of the *Silverado Gazette*. Nothing of local importance on the front page. Good. Maybe today would be an easy day.

When Jill opened the paper to page two, her own face stared back at her. She grimaced. She would never get used to seeing her campaign ads.

The November general election was the first in which Jill was officially running for sheriff. She'd been appointed to her post by the County Commissioners three years ago after Cory Fairmont retired.

Although she'd been Cory's chief deputy, she only got the job because Cory had thrown his considerable support behind her. Women might hold positions of power in boardrooms across the country, but in Silverado County the good old boy system still chugged right along. Men held all the important elected positions in the county—all except Jill's.

She'd spent the last three years making positive changes in the way things were done in the Sheriff's Department. The "no beer" policy at the bonfire was one. She'd instituted a zero tolerance policy for drunk drivers, no matter whose buddy they were.

She'd set also up the Secret Witness program that

the County Commissioners didn't think was necessary and funded it by trimming overtime out of her office budget. She knew she was the right person for the job. She just had to convince the voters.

The election was a little less than four weeks away, and her own chief deputy was running against her. While Jill thought Oren Michaelson would make a good sheriff if the people elected him, she didn't want to lose.

Someone sat down around the corner of the counter while Jill was scanning the local section, looking for anything of interest. She lowered the paper.

"He's back again," Hal Taylor said without preamble. "Can't you do something about that?"

Jill didn't have to ask who was back or where he was. She'd had this conversation with Hal Taylor too many times to count.

The "he" was Jeremiah Corbitt, seventy years old and one of Cumberland's crankiest senior citizens. Jeremiah was convinced that Hal, owner of Happy Hal's Cumberland Dodge, cheated him on a car repair job.

Most people would have written a few letters, maybe filed a complaint, and left it at that. Jeremiah

Corbitt wasn't most people. When the letters didn't work, Jeremiah decided to stage his own one-man protest by picketing Hal's business.

In the grand scheme of things, a one-man picket line was little more than an annoyance. Except a persistent old man with a picket sign didn't make Happy Hal very happy, and an annoyed Hal Taylor was a thorn in Jill's side that she didn't need at seven-thirty in the morning.

Hal was the closest thing Cumberland had to a celebrity. He'd turned the one used car lot he'd inherited from his father into four new and used car dealerships. His goofy television commercials featuring Happy Hal and his sidekick, Hal's general manager Stan "Sad Sack" Schmidt, aired on the local television channels in both Cumberland and Reno more often than reality shows. Hal Taylor drew a lot of business to the area, and that made every business owner in Cumberland a Happy Hal fan.

Hal had been a senior in Cumberland High when Jill was a freshman, and the intervening decades had been kind to him. He hadn't been conventionally handsome back then, but he'd had more than enough charm to make up for it.

These days the lines around his mouth and

creasing his forehead merely enhanced his rough features. His skin was a healthy tan year round. His black hair had gone salt and pepper in the way that made men look distinguished and women just look old. His shoulders were still broad like they'd been when he played football, and he hadn't let the rest of his muscles go to fat like so many former athletes did. He had a smile he could turn on at a moment's notice, and unlike many people who smiled for a living, Hal's smile reached and warmed his dark eyes. It was a good trait not only for a car salesman but for a politician, which probably explained why Hal was in his fourth term as County Commissioner.

In Cumberland, Hal Taylor had clout, and he wasn't above using it.

"Is Jeremiah on your property?" Jill asked Hal without closing the paper.

"He's at the Shell station across the street. Greg's not about to kick him off. He's got a soft spot for the old coot. I don't. He's not good for business."

Each time Hal complained, Jill sent out a deputy to roust Jeremiah, and each time Jeremiah promised to take his complaints to an attorney. Then a week or so later he'd show up again with another sign. He was smart enough never to set foot on Hal's property, so

Jill couldn't arrest him for trespassing.

Unfortunately for Hal, the business owners where Jeremiah chose to picket, like Greg Seaborn who owned the Shell station across the street from Hal's Dodge dealership, saw him as harmless and let him wave his homemade picket signs at passing motorists to his heart's content.

"What, exactly, do you want me to do?" Jill asked. "He's not on your property, Greg's not going to kick him off his. Why can't you just fix his problem and send him away happy?"

Hal looked at her like she was a particularly disgusting form of insect life.

"Because we didn't cause his problem. I'm not about to start fixing—for free, mind you—every knock and ping in every ten-year-old Dodge in this valley, which is what will happen if I fix his car out of the goodness of my heart."

Tina interrupted them with Jill's breakfast. She filled Hal's coffee cup from the pot she carried in one hand.

"You having anything to eat this morning, Hal?" she asked.

Jill noticed that Tina smiled a little more for Hal, even put a little flirtatious lilt in her voice. Hal had that effect on women.

"No thanks, babe," Hal said, smiling back like he hadn't been annoyed just a moment ago. "Just coffee."

Hal's habit of calling women "babe" annoyed Jill, but Tina didn't seem to mind. She also didn't seem to mind that Hal was married. A plain gold wedding band was prominent on the ring finger of his left hand.

"If you change your mind, just let me know." Tina stuck her pad back in the deep front pocket of her apron and walked out into the diner proper, circulating among the tables and refilling coffee cups as she went.

"Cory would have done something," Hal said as he stirred a packet of sugar into his coffee. He didn't look at Jill. "So would Oren."

So far Hal hadn't endorsed Jill or Oren even though everyone knew Hal and Oren were long-time buddies. The whole campaign, outside of a few bill-boards and newspaper ads, had been rather low key. Apparently Hal thought he could manipulate Jill by threatening to throw his support behind her opponent.

"You sure you want to go there, Hal?" she said. "Over something like this?"

Jill had seen Hal throw his clout around during County Commission meetings, and she'd heard gossip that he'd used his influence and resources in much less savory ways as well. The gossip stopped short of actually accusing Hal of illegal activities, but Jill never forgot that Happy Hal had a darker side he didn't let the general public see.

"I just want to drive to work and not see him out in front of my business with those signs of his. It's bad for business, and it's bad for the town's image. Why can't you see that?"

Jill put her fork down on her plate. "Get a restraining order against him. He violates it, I'll arrest him."

"That would take too long."

It would also give Jeremiah his day in court, and the local press would probably be there. Jeremiah with another protest sign didn't even merit a page five mention in the newspaper anymore, but Jeremiah going up against Happy Hal in court might even entice a news crew from Reno if they were having a slow news day.

"Look." Hal rubbed at his forehead. "Why don't you go talk to him? Your deputies go out and he gets his back up. You might have more luck with him. You're good with people, Jill, you always have been. Even when we were kids, you seemed to know how to connect with people."

Now he was flattering her. Pulling out all the big guns.

It never ceased to amaze her how in a town the size of Cumberland, small things became big things that had to be handled Right Now. Jeremiah Corbitt was clearly Hal Taylor's current big thing. Cory had warned Jill she'd have to play politics in this job. One of the people she had to play politics with was Hal Taylor. That didn't mean she had to like it.

Jill sighed and glanced at the neon-lit Coca-Cola clock on the back wall of the diner. The angle where she was sitting made it difficult to see precisely what time it was, but Jill could tell close enough. She didn't want to look at her watch; that was too obvious.

A mound of paperwork awaited her at her office, including the departmental budget report. She'd have just enough time to go talk to Jeremiah if she left soon.

"I'll go this one time," she said. "Next time, get a restraining order or I'm not sending anyone. Are we clear on that?"

Hal smiled, the same big grin he normally reserved for his television commercials. He thought he'd won, and maybe he had.

Jill didn't feel like she'd lost, though. Keeping the peace was her job. Talking to an angry old man was just one small part of it.

"Thanks, babe," Hal said. He finished the rest of his coffee, put a couple of dollar bills next to the empty cup, and stood up.

"Hal?" When he looked at her, Jill said, "Don't call me that. I prefer my name. I think you'll find most women do."

The look on his face said he didn't believe it. "You're okay, Jill." He gave her a mock salute with one finger and left the diner.

Great. She had the stamp of approval from Hal Taylor. Her day just couldn't get any better than that.

A Death
in
Cumberland

is currently available in both

paperback and all e-book formats

ABOUT THE AUTHOR

Annie Reed describes herself as a desert rat who longs to live by the ocean. Born and raised in Nevada, Annie started her writing career in science fiction. She soon branched out to fantasy, mystery, and crime fiction.

Annie still lives in Northern Nevada with her husband and daughter, who share their house with a number of high-maintenance cats. A friend to backyard bunnies and kamikaze quail, Annie would probably befriend dogs, too, except they'd chase the rabbits.

To find out more about Annie, visit www.annie-reed.com.

www.ingramcontent.com/pod-product-compliance
Lightning Source LLC
Chambersburg PA
CBHW032002240626
47153CB00003B/1087